RING AROUND A HAILSTONE

▼

Ring Around a Hailstone

▼

Bruce Salen

iUniverse.com, Inc.
San Jose New York Lincoln Shanghai

Ring Around A Hailstone

Published by iUniverse.com, Inc.

For information address:
iUniverse.com, Inc.
5220 S 16th, Ste. 200
Lincoln, NE 68512
www.iuniverse.com

ISBN: 0-595-14799-2

Printed in the United States of America

ACKNOWLEDGEMENTS

"Special thanks to Bob Rosen, whose brain-storming led to 'Barad's' creation, and to Paul Kaplan, whose friendship, support, and brain-storming helped in 'Barad's' development."

"Special thanks, also, to Bruce and Doris Bozarth for their invaluable proofreading and critiquing."

CHAPTER I

▼

THE TRAIN

The train stood on a little-used siding in the railroad yard in Dover, New Jersey. A lone figure stood in one of the sleeper compartments, deep in thought, as pale sunlight filtered through its winter-frosted windows.

The walls of the compartment were covered with poster-sized photos of Tel Dan, in northern Israel, the first dig he had worked on as a volunteer, many years before.

Eliezer Jordan drew a deep breath, and let it out slowly. For a minute or two, he studied his immediate surroundings.

"That was one hell of a dream," he thought, as he stretched his limbs. "Having a dream like that once is enough—but four times in two weeks? There must be some-thing to it. Let me see if I can learn anything."

So saying, he got a tubular container from a corner of the room, opened it, and took out a manuscript. He unrolled it, and placed it on the bed. After turning on an audio-cassette player, he picked up a small, hand-shaped pointer, moved it across the manuscript, and began to read.

The music of Smetana played softly in the background as he studied the manuscript. It was the Zohar, one of the most revered works of the Jewish mystical tradition. He was reading the portion known as the Secret of Secrets.

Patiently, he read on. As he did, a faint smile came to his face. It was as though a voice that only he could hear—a vision that only he could see—was assuring him that the answer to his riddle would soon be found.

Jordan suddenly remembered the day and time. "I'd better get a move on. I'm teaching two classes at the university this afternoon."

He rolled up the manuscript and returned it to its con-tainer. Then, he shut the cassette player, left his compart-ment, and went to the parlor car.

At one end of the car hung a hand-drawn poster illustrating an ancient Egyptian funerary scene, 'The Weighing of the Heart.' At the other end were two large posters—one of a breaching California Grey Whale, and one of some spinner dolphins. Along the walls were photos of plants and animals from around the world.

He was preparing a snack when a low, melodious chime sounded. Someone was calling him on the phone whose number was known to only five trusted friends. Each respected him enough to abide by his wish that they call that number only in an emergency. What problem did one of them have that might require his special knowledge and insights?

He stopped his work, and returned to his compartment. "Yes? What is it?" he asked, after picking up the phone.

"Prof. Jordan—Sean Ferguson speaking," said a voice with a trace of a soft Scottish burr.

The sound of that voice, and the mention of the name, reminded Jordan of their first meeting, two years earlier. He had been at a scholarly meeting in London. A mutual friend had introduced him to the Scot, who was investigating the theft of Arthurian relics from an ancient British bar-row—an investigation, which soon involved Jordan himself.

"Ahh–Ins. Ferguson. It's good to hear from you," said Jordan, heartily. "It's been quite some time. What's on your mind?" he asked, coming directly to the point. "What could have happened that might require an archaeologist's atten-tion?"

"I don't know if the archaeologist would be interested in my case. But I'm sure that the Kabbalist might want to look into it."

That in itself was enough to intrigue him. As a student of the Kabbalah, the ancient Jewish mystical tradition, Jordan had earned a rep-utation that rivaled his already considerable renown as an archaeologist and Biblical scholar. He had made a name for himself by his mastery of that tradition, and by his ability to use it to unravel mysteries that others had given up as beyond solving. And he was as well known by that name—the Hebrew word, Barad, meaning 'Hailstone'—as he was by the name he had been given at birth.

"It's a matter of murder," said the caller, likewise coming quickly to the point.

"Murder? Whose? When? Where? Can you give me any details?"

"Very few over the phone, I'm afraid. It has all the markings of another 'Ripper' affair. But I can't help thinking that there is more to it than that—much more".

"A homicidal maniac, perhaps?" Jordan thought, though he was certain that Ferguson would not have called if the case were not out of the ordi-nary.

He stood in pensive silence for a minute. Then, "Very well, Mr. Ferguson. I'll be glad to help. Classes at the university end in three days. I'll make my flight reserva-tions at once, then call you back and give you the informa-tion."

CHAPTER 2

▼

FERGUSON AND KELLY

Five days after that phone-call, Eliezer Jordan was on a plane bound for London. But even before his journey began, events over which he had no control were taking place in England—events, which would soon involve him.

In the middle of September, and again in mid-October, rural England had been plagued by a series of murders, which ended as suddenly and as mysteriously as they had begun.

Scotland Yard and the various local police forces were com-letely baffled. Despite their best efforts, and the availability of the latest scientific methods and facili-ties, the identity of their unknown adversary was still just that—unknown.

For the next two months, all was quiet. For two months, the press and the public were free to turn their attention to other matters—inflation, Ulster, unemployment, and in-creasing domestic unrest. For two months, the memory of those murders was out of the public's mind. But it was not out of the minds of the victims' families, or the two detectives who were leading the investigation.

Sunday, December 14, was an overcast day in London. The air was bone-chilling. For several days, the gray sky had been threatening to cover the city with snow, or drench it in icy rain. It was the sort of weather for which London is famous—or infamous, depending upon your health, or frame of mind.

Sean Ferguson was in very sound health, and in a fairly pleasant frame of mind, as he went to work this day.

Ferguson had an inquiring mind, and an interest in many things. He also had a talent for storing obscure and trivial facts in his memory, sifting through them, and using them in the right combination on the right occasion.

But thus far, neither this ability, nor his tenacity, nor his devotion to duty, had been of much avail on his latest case. After three months, he was hopelessly stalemated.

"Ferguson—where have you been?" his friend and col-league, Inspector John Kelly, greeted him, when he entered his office.

"By the Embankment, watching the boats. You know, Kelly, if I hadn't become a nemesis of evildoers, I should like to have been master of a schooner."

"Well, you may still have the chance."

"Really? How?"

"The Chief's been fuming all morning. He wants to see us. It's begun again," he said.

There was no need to ask what 'it' was.

"Where was the body found?" Ferguson asked.

"Bodies," Kelly grimly corrected him. "Two, to be precise. One at London Wall, and one in St. Paul's Cathedral."

"Whoever he is, he's getting bold," the Scot noted. "Assuming, of course, that it's the same bastard who com-mitted the other murders."

"It's the same one, alright. Same type of wounds, and just as devilishly clean as the others."

A moment later, they reached their destination. Kelly knocked on the door. A voice within bade him enter.

"Damnation, Ferguson!" snapped Chief Inspector Oswald, when he saw them. "Where have you been all morning?!"

"It's barely eight o'clock, sir," said Ferguson, looking at the small clock on the desk. "I've just come on duty. Kelly has just told me the news."

"Yes. Our blood-thirsty friend is at it again."

Ferguson walked slowly to the window. Like Kelly, he was angered by the return of their anonymous adversary—by this renewed threat to public safety, and by their failure to bring the fiend to justice.

Chief Inspector Oswald, too, was upset—by the audacity of the killer, and by his skill at eluding the police.

"Well?! What do you intend to do?!" he demanded.

"Do?" asked a surprised Kelly. "Why, we intend to solve the case. I thought you knew that," he replied, with his characteristic nonchalance and bluntness.

"We can begin by going to Forensics," Ferguson suggested to his friend. "We'll read their report, and then go to the hospital, to see the bodies. Then we'll visit the scenes of the crimes, and call on the families of the victims."

Kelly nodded in ready agreement.

"Let's be off, then," said the Scot. "We've much to do."

With that, the two men turned and left.

CHAPTER 3

▼

FERGUSON AND JORDAN

The plane landed, and taxied to the appropriate gate. After coming to a halt, its door opened. Its passengers emerged, and made their way to the areas marked BAGGAGE and CUSTOMS.

Eliezer Jordan claimed his two duffel bags. One con-tained his cloth-ing, and the other held his Kabbalistic 'tool-kit'—a blue terry-cloth robe, a brown woolen skull-cap, and a beige woolen prayer-shawl; a small cas-sette-player, and two audiocassettes with music that he had chosen for his own rather unconventional task.

A few minutes later, he had a visitor's visa stamped in his passport. Hundreds of other people were doing the same when he heard a familiar voice paging him. He turned.

"Mr. Ferguson—good to see you again. And to have an official recep-tion," he said, as they shook hands.

"It was the least I could do," said the detective. "After all, you were good enough to come here on such short notice—even though I told you so little when I rang."

"You were rather brief on the phone," Jordan replied. "Now, would you care to fill me in on the details?"

"Yes—as soon as we get to the Yard," the Scot answered, as they left the terminal building and walked to his car. An hour later, they turned a corner, and came to a stop in front of the Ferguson residence.

After a shower, shave, and change of clothes, Jordan felt ready to tackle the problem that had brought him to England. Without delay, he and Ferguson drove to Scotland Yard, and went up to the detective's office.

"Three months ago, there were two murders—one in Bod-min, and one in Tavistock," Ferguson began. "That was on 5 September. A week later, on the eleventh, there were three more—one near Glastonbury; one near Keevil; and one near Westbury. All were horribly mutilated in some way."

Jordan grimaced. "What can you tell me about the wounds?" he asked. "Were they clean? Or messy?"

Ferguson took a deep breath. "Clean as a whistle," he said. "A second series of murders began in mid-October," he continued, after a brief pause. "On the 18th, there was one near Chipping-Norton. Ten days later, there were two more, both at Brocolitia, an old Roman temple at Hadrian's Wall."

"Do you have a map of Britain handy?" Jordan asked. "I'd like to know where these places are. Except for the Wall, they're all just names to me."

The detective took a motorists' map from a drawer of his desk, unfolded it, and fastened it to the wall. He then drew his friend's attention to the sites of the murders.

"After the two deaths at the Wall, there was nothing until this past Sunday, three days after I rang you. This time, two bodies were found right here in London—one at London Wall, and one in St. Paul's Cathedral."

"And all killed in the same manner?"

The man nodded. "Kelly and I have already seen the bodies. We've spoken with Forensics, and read their report. I still have it, if you care to see it."

Jordan took the manila folder, and read the report. When he finished,
he closed it, and returned it to his friend. Then, he questioned him about
the investigation.

"What have you learned?" he asked. "Is there a connec-tion?"

"Thus far, nothing that we can see. You're assuming, of course, that
there might be some thread tying the victims together. It's a possibility, of
course."

"I know. It's something to be considered, though not taken for
granted," Jordan noted. "The fact that several people were killed in the
same manner implies the same murderer. It doesn't mean that the victims
knew each other—or their killer."

Ferguson then handed Jordan a second folder.

"This covers of our investigation right from the begin-ning," he said.
"It starts with the discovery of the first victim, three months ago. The
entries for the two latest victims are still minimal—physical description;
time and cause of death; date and time of discovery."

Jordan nodded understandingly. He then skimmed through this second
report. Here and there, he paused, and jotted down some notes on a small
pad. When he finished, he rubbed his face, as if trying to wipe away the
image that the report had conjured up in his mind.

"Are you familiar with rail service in Britain?" he then
asked, apparently changing the subject.

"Of course. Why?"

"I'd like to visit the scenes of the crimes. I want to see the areas for
myself—perhaps speak with people who knew the victims."

"Is that really necessary? You'd be going over ground that had already
been examined—by the local police, and by Kelly and myself. Besides,
don't these two reports tell you what you need to know?"

"They're both very helpful," Jordan assured him. "But I'd like to see and
feel the scenes of the crimes for myself. If I'm going to be of any real help to

you, I'll have to do more than just read an official report, no matter how good it is. A personal visit will let me see things from my own perspective."

Ferguson took a slow, deep breath. Then, he removed a thick book from his desk, and began to flip through it.

"Here we are. There's a train leaving Paddington Station for Penzance at four this afternoon. And one tomorrow morning at 8:10. Which would you prefer?"

"The 8:10 sounds good. Why don't I go to Paddington now get train tickets, maybe arrange for renting a car, as well? Then I'll phone you, and let you know what I've done."

Ferguson nodded. "Very well," he said, as they left the office, and walked to the elevator. For the first time in three months, he began to feel that he could now meet his unseen adversary on even terms. "If Kelly and I can help you in any way, please let us know," he emphasized.

"Did I hear my name mentioned?" a voice behind them asked. They turned, and saw a lean figure walking towards them.

"Prof. Jordan—how nice to see you," John Kelly greeted him. "Even if it is under unpleasant circumstances.

The two men exchanged warm handshakes, as the newcomer informed Ferguson that Chief Inspector Oswald wanted to see them in his office.

"I'll be on my way, then, gentlemen," said Jordan. "I don't want to keep you from your meeting. I'll be talking with you within the hour."

CHAPTER 4

▼

A VISITOR

"Well? What have you and Jordan been up to?" Kelly asked. "Have you made any headway?"

"Headway? Of course not. How could we? After all, he got here only this morning. Even he is human. By the way, what does the Chief want, now?" he asked.

"I don't know. I bumped into him but a moment ago—he said that he wanted the both of us in his office, without delay."

Arriving at Oswald's office, they knocked on the door.

Without waiting for a response, Kelly opened it and entered, followed by his friend. Two other men, one of them a police constable, had already proceeded them there.

"Constable Fitzwilliams came across this fellow in Hyde Park a short while ago," Oswald told them. "He may need our help—yours, at any rate."

"Who is he? What does he want?" asked Kelly.

"That's what I want to know. He seems to speak no English. He was stopping people and asking for something, but in a language that nobody understands."

Oswald then reached for a book that was lying on his desk. "This is why he was brought here, and why I sent for you."

Ferguson and Kelly were genuinely mystified. They looked at each other, then at Oswald and the stranger, not knowing what to expect.

"He was carrying this," Oswald went on. "There's some-thing written inside, along with a letter addressed to the two of you. He brought three copies of this book, actually—one for each of you, and one for someone named Eliezer Jordan. Who is he?"

"He's a very good friend of ours," said Kelly. "I'm sure he'll appreciate this unexpected gift."

He took the book from Oswald, opened it, and began to skim through it. When he finished, their silent visitor found his voice. Neither Oswald nor Ferguson understood him, but John Kelly obviously did.

They spoke for several minutes in animated tones. Kelly turned to the others, and spoke in English.

"Constable, I must thank you for bringing this man here. He's come from St. Ives, to give us this old edition of the Mabinogion."

"The Mabi-what? What is that?" asked Oswald.

"The Mabinogion," Kelly calmly repeated. "It's a collec-tion of eleven medieval Welsh tales which first appeared in the eleventh century—the most prominent result of a flow-ering of Welsh prose. They tell us many of the cultic legends of pagan Britain. You mean you didn't know?"

"A book of fairy tales?" asked an incredulous Oswald. "He came here from St. Ives just to give you a book of fairy tales?"

"Wrong on both counts, sir," Kelly replied. "These legends are by no means children's stories, or 'fairy tales'. They're part of Britain's ancient culture—the creation and heritage of its Celtic inhabitants. And his visit, and this gift, have a purpose."

"And what would that be, I wonder? Why would anyone inscribe a book of Welsh legends to the two of you, or to this Jordan fellow? Or travel from St. Ives, to deliver it personally."

"Do you recall that case we worked on in Tintagel, two years ago?" Kelly asked his two colleagues.

"Quite well," Ferguson replied. "It's amazing what one can find in those old barrows. Why?"

"Cardigan and I were speaking the language of the ancient Celts. He belongs to a group dedicated to reviving and preserving their ancient Celtic heritage—art, music, literature, language, etc. He and his friends wanted to give us this copy of the Mabinogion as a token of gratitude for work at Tintagel, and our rescue of its Arthurian relics."

"That's rather nice of them," said Ferguson, with a sincere surprise and modesty. "But we can't accept gifts from everyone who appreciates our work, can we? After all, it's a question of professional ethics."

CHAPTER 5

▼

JOHN KELLY'S EXUBERANCE

John Kelly was beside himself with joy, as he and Ferguson entered their office with their visitor. Careful-ly, almost reverently, he placed the gift on his desk, and opened it with care. With a sense of genuine admiration, he viewed the hand-drawn title page.

He was unusually excited. And, as was sometimes the case, he was beginning to drive his friend to distraction.

"Have you forgotten that we have a more pressing matter to deal with?" Ferguson reminded him. "That our case is still unsolved?"

Kelly looked at him. "Ferguson, you've cut me to the quick. You should know that duty and I are never far apart," he said.

Ferguson chuckled. "No one knows of your devotion to duty better than I. But you seem to have forgotten that a murder-er is still running around scot-free—a murderer who has successfully eluded us for the past three months."

Kelly shrugged his shoulders and sighed.

"No, I haven't forgotten," he assured his friend. "And I'm sure that our anonymous friend will slip up, sooner or later."

"Well, at least someone is confident that he will. I was beginning to have some misgivings."

Kelly smiled. "I know. So was I. But it's precisely at a time like this—when we're on a baffling case, and both the tension and frustration seem unbearable—that we need just such a diversion."

Ferguson filled and lit his pipe. He looked at his friend, then at their visitor, and considered his words.

"Perhaps you're right," he said. "Perhaps a brief diversion is needed. But I can't understand why you should wax poetic over a book of old legends," he added, as he rose from his seat, and walked over to his friend and their guest.

"Come now, Ferguson—haven't you ever been thrilled by the exploits of Pwyll, Lord of the Seven Cantrefs of Dyfed? Nor ever shed a tear over the sad plight of Branwen, daughter of Llyr?"

"No, I haven't. In fact, I never heard of either of them until this moment. Nor had I ever heard of the Mabinogion, or seen a copy of it, until today."

Kelly shook his head. "I suppose you've never addressed your wife as Rigantona," he said, in a tone of mock anger.

"Just who, or what, might Rigantona be?"

"Don't you know? The name is Celtic, my dear fellow. It means 'Great Queen Goddess.' Don't you think Peggy would like to be addressed as 'Divine Queen'?" he asked, as they enjoyed a hearty laugh.

"Once or twice—perhaps," thought Ferguson. "But it would soon wear out its welcome, I'm afraid. Peggy isn't one to tolerate such flattery for very long—even if it is from me," he said, with a smile.

Ferguson returned to his desk, and his work. Kelly was about to do the same, when something caught his eye as he turned the pages of the book.

"Well, hello, Mrs. MacFarland!" he exclaimed. His face lit up as he called his friend. "Ferguson, come here. Have a look at this, will you?"

"Damn this infernal interference!" Ferguson grumbled. "We'll never get any work done, at this rate."

Then, aloud, "Well? What have you found? It must be out of the ordinary—you would never address the mythical Mrs. MacFarland if it were commonplace."

"Look for yourself," Kelly replied. Excitedly, he drew his friend's attention to three specific pages.

"Well?" said the latter. "All I see are two maps of Britain, and a page with oddly-shaped circles." The exasperated detective began to whistle Loch Lommond, as he tried to defuse his rising temper.

Kelly was about to explain the meaning of the maps, and of the peculiar diagrams, when the phone rang. "Yes? Kelly here," he answered.

"Kelly? It's Jordan. I'm at Paddington. I'll be a bit delayed on my way back to you. No, nothing serious—I just thought that I'd pay a brief visit to the Jewish Museum."

"Very well," said the detective. "But I hope that the delay won't be too long. We have a visitor—from St. Ives. He's eager to meet you."

"Really? Who is it?"

"Do you remember that case at Tintagel, two years ago?"

"Yes. That's how we first met. Well?"

"That's why he came to see us—and why he wants to see you," Kelly told him.

"Hmm. Well, you've aroused my curiosity. I'll be right there."

CHAPTER 6

▼

AT PADDINGTON STATION

There was a brisk chill in the air as Eliezer Jordan left Scotland Yard, and took the underground to Paddington Station. He made his way up to street level, and walked through the station to the ticket office.

He bought his train ticket, then went to the information office, to inquire about renting a car. He browsed through the assorted brochures.

"May I help you?" a clerk asked.

"Yes. I'd like to travel to Cornwall and Devonshire. Have you any information on hotels and car-hires?"

"Yes, we do. Let me see," the clerk offered.

He removed some fliers from the stand behind him, and gave them to Jordan. "Here you are, sir. An RAC map; information on car-hires; and a list of hotels and guests-houses in Cornwall and Devon. Have you any particular places in mind?"

"No—nothing definite at the moment, I'm afraid."

Jordan then looked at the map. "Going by train to Plymouth, and hiring a car there, sounds like a good idea," he finally said. "I think I'll do that. Can I take these brochures?"

"Of course."

Jordan turned to leave, then paused. "By the way," he asked, "is it possible to reserve a car in Plymouth, from here? And a room in a guesthouse, as well?"

"Yes. One of those brochures will help you with car hire. Another has a list of guesthouses in Devon and Cornwall, with addresses and phone-numbers. Is there anything else?"

"Yes—one more thing, if you don't mind. Have you any railway timetables? Not only for Cornwall, but for the rest of England, as well?"

"This is all I have, at the moment. If you need others, you might check the rack on the wall."

"Good. Many thanks."

Jordan followed the man's advice. Then, he raised his hand to open the door when, as if by accident, he spotted a small object on the floor.

"Hmm. I wonder what it is," he thought, as his curiosity prompted him to pause, and pick it up. It looked like some sort of small marble. On each side, it bore strange, unfamiliar markings.

"Someone must have lost it," he decided. "These markings are intriguing. Could they mean anything?" He turned it around, then put it in his pocket, and went off to buy his ticket.

"What now?" he thought, when that was done. "Yeah—hire a car, and pick it up in Plymouth. And reserve a room in a guesthouse."

So saying, he then made the necessary arrangements.

His immediate business taken care of, he now stood in the middle of the waiting room of the huge terminal. "What now?" he wondered. "Back to the Yard?"

He looked at a clock—it was 2:27. "It's been quite a busy day, so far," he thought, as he put his hands into the pockets of his jacket. "I'd like to see the Jewish Museum. Let me call Ferguson, and let him know what I've decided."

His call was soon answered by a voice with a familiar accent, a peculiar blend of singsong Yiddish and melodious Irish brogue.

"Yes? Kelly speaking."

"Kelly? Jordan here. At Paddington. I'll be slightly delayed on my way back to you. No, nothing's wrong. I want to stop at the Jewish Museum. A visitor? With a gift? Tintagel? Yes, I remember. Very well—I'm on my way."

CHAPTER 7

▼

THE FIVE CIRCLES

"That was Jordan," said Kelly, when he put the phone down. "Calling from Paddington. He's on his way back."

"Good," was Ferguson's only comment, as he tried to concentrate on his work.

Kelly, the meanwhile, was studying his copy of Cardigan's book. Then, with no particular thoughts in mind, he found himself gazing, almost hypnotically, at the two pages he had shown the Scot.

"Hmm. Very curious," he mumbled. "Very curious, indeed. And very interesting," he added, as he slowly and deliber-ately moved his fingers around the pages that had originally excited him.

The book's hold on his attention was broken by the ring-ing of his phone, then a knock on the door a few minutes later. The door opened, and Jordan entered.

"Well, gentlemen," he said. "Would you care to tell me who your guest is? And why he wants to see me?

Kelly answered his questions with unusual brevity. "I was about to draw Ferguson's attention to something, when you rang," he concluded. "It's quite interesting."

With a wave of his hand, he showed Jordan the drawings that had gotten him so excited a short while earlier.

With a healthy curiosity, and a regard for detail, Jordan studied the drawings carefully. It was obvious to the detectives that their friend's professional instincts had been aroused. Though his areas of specialization didn't include Britain, he suspected that these were no ordinary drawings.

With Kelly's help, Jordan told the Cornishman, "This is a kind and generous gift, Mr. Cardigan; and very unexpected. I can't thank you and your friends enough. The three of us were only too glad to help on that case," he said, as he and Cardigan exchanged warm smiles and handshakes.

"But what are those drawings?" asked Ferguson, his curiosity still unsatisfied.

"Oh—the drawings. That's easy enough to explain," Kelly replied. "This one has five circles of different shapes—a true circle; flattened circle; ellipse; egg-shaped circle; and compound ring. They represent the five general shapes of the megalithic rings of Britain. Underneath each one is an outline of an actual stone circle—an example of that category."

"And the two maps?"

"This one shows the distribution of stone circles in Britain and Ireland, with important sites named—Avebury, Stanton Drew, and Stonehenge, for example. The second map is a bit more detailed. It shows the henges and great stone circles, and indicates four types of structures—stone circles, henges, circle henges, and circles around a cairn, or burial chamber."

Ferguson was at a loss for words. Gifts always made him feel self-conscious—this one even more so, because it came as a result of his work on one case, and interrupted his work on another. Sensing his friend's feeling, Jordan offered a helpful suggestion.

"You fellows have more important things to do, right now, than look at a book of old legends. If you don't mind, Mr. Cardigan and I will leave you for awhile. We'll return when you're off duty."

"Very well," the detectives agreed. "But what are you going to do for the next four hours?" Kelly wondered. "How will you communicate? You don't speak Gaelic, do you?"

"No, I'm afraid not," Jordan confessed, as he put on his coat.

"And I doubt that he speaks Hebrew, Aramaic, or Akkadi-an." He shrugged his shoulders, then said, "Don't worry. We'll find a way to bridge the gaps of language and culture."

So saying, he and Cardigan left, allowing Ferguson and Kelly to get back to more serious matters.

CHAPTER 8

▼

NAGGING QUESTIONS

With a seriousness that surprised even Ferguson, John Kelly rose from his seat. He looked at his friend.

"I've rarely ever seen you wear such a somber expression," said the Scot. "Is anything wrong?"

"Wrong? No—aside from this devilish case, that is. It may well be that we already have a solution to these horrible crimes in our possession. It might be something so obvious—so ordinary—that we've simply over-looked it."

He rubbed his tired face, as if trying to wipe something away.

Try though he might, he could not erase his fatigue, or his frustration. Neither his gesture, nor the diversion caused by Cardigan and his gift, could erase the memory of the hard work and sleepless nights, or the hor-rible condition of the victims.

John Kelly remembered them. He shook his head, but the memories, and the frustration, remained.

"I think I'll follow my advice to you," he finally said. "A large mug of herbal tea, with a dash of honey. And then—what?"

"And then? A call on the mythical Mrs. MacFarland, perhaps?" asked Ferguson.

"Mrs. MacFarland is by no means mythical," Kelly was quick to point out. "She is as real as you and I. While not a criminal herself, she does have numerous contacts in the London underworld. And she has been a source of valuable information for me for both of us—on many of our cases."

"It seems odd, then, that with such a source of information to draw upon, we've learned nothing."

"It is. But it's not from lack of effort, I can assure you. And that effort will continue," Kelly said, indicating the folder he was holding. "I'll be in the library, if you need me. I feel the need to review this case very slowly, and very deliberately."

"'I want to be alone'. Is that it? Very well, Kelly. As you wish."

After his friend left, Ferguson slowly got up out of his seat. He looked at the file that lay open on his desk. Then, turning away from the data that he knew by heart, he decided to heat up a mug of his friend's herbal tea.

He sipped his drink. Its flavor was enhanced by a pinch of cinnamon. Its warmth contrasted sharply with the chill outside. He gazed through the window, out over the damp, cloud-covered metropolis, and wondered why Kelly chose to go to the library. What did he plan to do, that they had not already done? What could he hope to find, that three months of hard work and sleepless nights by four police forces had not brought to light?

As he watched the scene before him, other questions came to mind. How would Jordan and Cardigan spend the day? How would they communicate, since they shared no common language? Could Jordan, with his special knowledge, provide the perspective that could help them solve this case?

Then came the recurring questions—the ones that nagged him, like a bad dream that refused to go away. Who was this anonymous killer? What was the method to his destructive madness? Was there a method? How and why had he chosen his victims? Where is my elusive quarry at this moment? What is he doing, whilst I'm trying to soothe my nerves with a cup of Kelly's home-brewed ginseng tea?

CHAPTER 9

▼

BY NORWOOD GREEN

The answers to some of Ferguson's questions were to be found in a flat only a few miles from his office. A Persian carpet covered much of the sitting-room floor. Two walls held paintings and photos of rustic rural scenes. They conveyed an idealized image of some long-gone, long forgotten age—a Golden Age peopled by Noble Savages, and which existed only in the fantasies of philosophers and poets, never in reality.

The third wall held hand-carved, book-lined shelves. The shelves were made of pine, as were the bookends. The books covered a variety of esoteric subjects—shamanism; astrology; Atlantis; the archaeology and prehistory of Britain and northern Europe; stone circles and henges; and parapsychology.

Another set of shelves lined the fourth wall. They held handmade replicas of prehistoric European artwork—the Gundestorp cauldron; torcs; Avebury; and figures of charac-ters from the various mythologies of pagan Europe.

A man and two women were in the room. One woman was seated on the sofa. A pair of strong, clear hazel eyes looked out from her handsome face. Her straight, auburn hair was combed in a pageboy style. Some balls of wool rested beside her. Her busy fingers nimbly knitted them into the beginnings of an afghan.

The second woman sat at a table by the window. Her curly, sandy-brown hair, and weather-beaten complexion, imparted a certain innocent, unspoiled aura to her features.

She held a clipboard, with several sheets of drawing paper, in her right hand. As she viewed the scene outside—almost hypnotically, it seemed—her left hand would reach down to a tray on a table. On that tray was a mug of steaming broth, and an assortment of colored pencils.

With an ease born of habit, and natural talent, she filled some of those pages with a series of superb scenes and sketches. As if under the spell of some power greater than herself, she continued to draw until she was satisfied with her work. Her eyes took in the scene outside, and her hand moved as if guided by a will of its own. But what she drew bore no resemblance to the scene outside that window.

The man in that room had spent his life close to the elements on a fishing boat; in tin times; and digging the soil of Cornwall and Devon for relics of Britain's long gone past. He had a certain aura about him—a magnetism that one could not fail to notice.

Quietly and carefully, his eyes and hands worked their way along each bookshelf. Now and then, he paused in his search. He would remove a book. With the air of one who knew precisely what he wanted, and where to find it, he proceeded to the desired parts of each volume.

For the better part of three hours, Andrew Barrett busied himself in this manner. In that time, he focused his atten-tion on ten of those books. Examining each one, in turn, until he found what he wanted, he then sat

down at an oaken desk. Removing a pen and writing pad from the center
drawer, he began to make some notes.

For three hours, neither Barrett, nor the two women with him, said a
word. For three hours, each of them was wrapped snuggly and comfort-
ably in his or her own little world.

At last, Nora Mulholland stopped her drawing. She placed her pad and
pencils on a table that stood in the middle of the room.

"Are you planning something, Andrew?" she asked, when she
noticed the board game that he had set up on the table—a game based
on the ancient Irish Book of Invasions.

"Yes. Why do you ask?"

Those were the first words that either of them had spoken all day.

"I'm simply curious, my dear filidh," was her simple answer. "After all,
the game is your own creation. And the Circle accepted it with some
enthusiasm. But I could not fail to notice that to you, it's something more
than a board-game."

"Of course it's more than just a game," Ellen Chatham emphatically
interrupted, without losing the rhythm of her knitting. "You surprise me,
Nora. You've always been one of the foremost conservators of our tradi-
tions. As well as anyone, you should know that the Book is one of our
most prized literary possessions."

"Yes, yes. I do," the artist replied, in a soft, silken voice. "I was merely
noticing a coincidence. I can't help thinking that whenever Andrew sets
up that board and its pieces, he's planning something—and the legends of
the Book seem to help him focus his attention."

Barrett stood up. Without a word, he went to the kitchen. He filled his
mug with some warm broth, then put some freshly baked biscuits onto a
small dish. Returning to the sitting room, he resumed his seat.

With a cursory glance, he looked at the books that he had been reading,
and the notes that he had made. As he did, he sipped the broth, and ate
one of the cookies.

"You're quite right, Nora," he finally replied, in a firm, quiet tone. "It is more than just a game to me. Just as the Mabinogion is more than an assortment of entertaining stories. In its own way, the Book represents what has happened to our race, our culture, our island."

"Does it, really?" she asked, a bit skeptically. "To be candid, I had never seen it that way. Why do you feel so strongly about it?"

Barrett drew a slow, deep breath, and frowned. "Haven't these islands been overrun by a succession of invaders and interlopers?" he replied, after a brief, tense silence.

"Romans, Anglo-Saxons, Danes, Normans—all have intruded themselves onto our land, depriving us of its wealth and sanctity, neutralizing its great aura," he continued. "They've imposed their rule and their ways upon us, until our own wondrous heritage has become a diluted, meaningless memory."

He looked at her with an air of self-importance, then finished his biscuits and broth. As he did, Nora studied him with care. "There will be more deaths, then," she said, half-asking, half knowing the answer, as she arranged her sketches.

Was she having second thoughts about her involvement with the Keepers of the Ley Lines? Feeling moral qualms about the revival of the Cult? Or questioning the decisions of their druid, Malcolm Morgan?

"A fair assumption, Nora," Barrett replied, as he closed his books, returned them to the shelves, and put his notes in order. "My dear girl," the normally silent, moody Ellen added. "You know full well that each of these deaths has served a noble purpose. Our land needs to be cleansed and purified. So do we, if we are ever to reclaim and retain the ancient paths."

So saying, she rose from the sofa, and speedily packed up her knitting. With her strong, forceful features, she some-how didn't look like the type who ever really could, or would, be content to while away her time with a task as peaceful as knitting.

She glanced at her watch. "Isn't it time to go to the Museum?" she reminded her companions. "What time is the talk, Andrew?"

"Three o'clock. That gives us two hours—ample time to stop at Paddington, and buy tickets for Penzance," he said. He then put his notes, and a packet of transparencies, into a canvas tote bag, and put on a warm coat, hat, and muffler.

Ellen put aside her bag of wool, and put on her heavy coat and scarf. And Nora put away her pastels and char-coals, placed her pad of life-like drawings into a blue portfolio, then bundled herself up in a green woolen glen-garry and a heavy tweed coat.

Had they forgotten anything? They looked quickly around the room. No—they had everything—all that they would need, for their talk at the British Museum.

CHAPTER 10

▼

SHIPS THAT PASS

The usual assortment of passengers got off the train, while others quickly boarded, and took their seats. The train was exceptionally crowded, as many riders were going to London to do some last-minute shopping. Three of the travelers, however, were bound for London with a very different purpose in mind.

When the train pulled into Paddington, and the end of its run, its riders disembarked, and went about their business.

In the middle of the waiting room, three of them paused. Andrew Barrett gazed in wonder at the great edifice around them.

"My word—this certainly is an impressive structure, isn't it? In all my trips to London, it's never failed to overwhelm me. Doesn't the architecture appeal to the artist in you, Nora?"

Looking about in a cursory manner, she casually replied, "Not in the slightest. It's tasteless—tasteless, and depressing." The man raised his eyebrows. Her reply sur-prised him. Then, with a shrug of his shoulders, he went with Ellen to the ticket office. Nora chose to go to the bookstore, to buy a newspaper and some magazines.

At that moment, the bookstore was one of the busiest parts of the huge terminal. As she opened the door, she accidentally bumped into a man who was just leaving.

The man walked briskly to the ticket office. He had entered soon after Andrew Barrett and Ellen Chatham had emerged; they had just brought three tickets to Penzance, and were now waiting for Nora to meet them.

The man took no notice of them, nor they of him. Nor did Barrett notice that he had dropped something in the ticket office. It was small and inconspicuous, and not really worth a second glance. Only by the merest chance did Eliezer Jordan see it lying there.

It looked almost like a marble—oval, with a flat bottom, and a pale, frosty gray in color. One side had a dark blue spot, surrounded by a dark gray circle. A white edge penetrated the spot, giving in the appearance of a pie with a very thin slice cut out of it.

"Hmm—I wonder what it is," Jordan asked himself, as he picked it up, and studied it. He turned it slowly around with the tips of his fingers, and examined it for a few seconds.

"Can't be a marble," he thought. "At least, it's not an American shooting marble. What is it? An ornament? Mm—peculiar little design in there. Looks like the pupil of a cat's eye. Wonder if it means anything. No matter—it's a cute little curiosity."

So saying, he put it in his shirt pocket, and went about his business. After a phone-call to his two friends, he returned to their office, high above Victoria Street.

As he made his way to one of London's most famous addresses, three other people went by underground to Russell Square, and another well-known structure. At Montague Street, they entered the busy, regal confines of the British Museum. They slackened their pace but slightly, stopping at the office of Thomas Richmond, Assistant Curator of Celtic and Anglo-Saxon Art.

Ellen knocked on the door four times, in rapid succession. Her knock was soon followed by the sound of a voice within, inviting them to enter.

With a hand whose pudginess belied its dexterity, she opened the door. Followed by her companions, she entered with the air of one who knew exactly what she wanted, and intended to get it.

"Mr. Richmond?" said the man with her. "I'm Andrew Barrett. I believe you're expecting me."

"Mr. Barrett? Yes—of course," Richmond replied. Putting aside his paperwork, he got up, and stepped forward to greet his visitors.

"Please sit down," he invited them. "Let me see—your lecture is at three o'clock. And you wanted two projectors, if I'm not mistaken—one for sketches, and one for trans-parencies."

"Correct. And we do appreciate your assistance," Barrett assured him. Taking one of the proffered seats, he draped his coat and scarf over one of its arms, and sat down.

Unbuttoning her coat, Ellen stood for a few minutes in the middle of the office. With her nose in the air, she surveyed her surroundings. Her all-too-obvious attitude was that of a woman who assumed that everyone and everything naturally waited with baited breath for her approval or dis-approval.

Her critical gaze scrutinized the office and its con-tents. Richmond's desk stood near the window, which over-looked snow-covered Bedford Square. A replica of the Gundestorp Cauldron sat on one corner. A painted model of the Sutton Hoo Viking ship, complete with sails and oars, was on the other. A few books and scholarly journals sat off to one side of the desk.

"Both are hand-made," said Richmond, in an effort to make con-versation, and make his guests feel at home. He was equally interested in his own peace of mind—his three visitors had entered his office with a smug, condescending air about them. Only a dullard would have failed to notice it, or react to it.

"I made them myself," he added, with a touch of good-natured pride. "Wood-carving and metal-craft are hobbies of mine. They call for a good deal of patience and concentration. But I find them very relaxing. And there's a considerable satisfaction, once I've completed something."

"Yes. I'm sure there is," said Barrett, dryly. Then, he turned their attention to the purpose of the visit.

"Tell me, Mr. Richmond, what steps have you taken to publicise today's talk?"

"The usual steps," Richmond replied. "We've sent notices to our members, and have posted them at various points throughout the Museum."

"Is that all? What of the various Royal Societies—Geographical? Astronomical? Archaeological? Or University Departments of Archaeology, and Astronomy? Not to mention individual scholars?"

"Mr. Barrett, by the time you begin your talk, several thousand people will have been informed of its time and place. We've extended ourselves by providing you with a room for your lecture, and telling our membership of it. That should suffice."

Barrett was unaccustomed to being spoken to in so blunt or forceful a manner. And he didn't like it.

Expressions of contempt came to the faces of Andrew Barrett and Ellen Chatham. If looks could kill, poor Mr. Richmond would have died then and there.

"I...see," said Barrett, controlling his temper with some effort.

A tense silence followed. Then, "If you don't mind, we would like to go to the room set aside for our presenta-tion," said Barrett.

The curator heaved a sigh of relief. He stood up, crossed the room, and opened the door. "This way," he said, grateful for this chance to relieve himself of his unwelcome guests.

CHAPTER 11

▼

A MATTER OF PERSPECTIVE

The two men emerged from the underground station at Tot-tenham Court Road, and walked to the British Museum. The cold, crisp air added vigor to their step.

They entered the Museum's begrimed yet stately portals, and checked their coats. Llewellyn Cardigan and Eliezer Jordan were pressed for time, and wanted to use the avail-able time as wisely as possible.

They walked passed various displays at an easy pace. Jordan's first desire was to visit the Egyptian, Assyrian, and Canaanite displays.

"No, not there," said Cardigan, speaking in the ancient Cornish dialect. "You've probably seen those works, and others like them, many times. I should like to show you something else—something different."

A puzzled look came to Jordan's face. It wasn't that he mistrusted the man—despite the language problem, he and Cardigan took a liking to each other from the start, and felt a comfortable rapport. With a shrug of his shoulders, Jordan followed the man, naturally wondering whither he would lead him.

"I'd like to show you something of my own heritage," said Cardigan. "I'd like to share it with you—to show you that my ancestors weren't the crude barbarians described by Caesar, Suetonius, and others."

There was something hauntingly familiar about the man's speech. It tantalized Jordan, piquing his curiosity no end. It was like the proverbial mosquito-bite between the shoulder blades, just where you can't reach it—the word on the tip of your tongue—the memory just beyond recall.

Prompted by his healthy curiosity, and by his interest in ancient languages, he now spoke to Cardigan. Knowing no Gaelic, he fell back on another resource, and spoke a language not used for twenty-five centuries.

"It's quite possible," he said. "Much of what they wrote is valuable to us, but all historians have their own prejudices, their own views and perspectives. It's true of every historian since Herodotus. And even he was no exception," he noted with a smile.

Cardigan raised his eyebrows, and looked at Jordan with an expression of pleasant surprise. "Indeed," he agreed.

"They all see what they want to see—and how they want to see it," Jordan continued. "And we're left with the task of seeking any grains of truth intertwined with their prejudices and exaggerations."

They soon reached the gallery housing the collection of prehistoric British art and artifacts. Proceeding slowly through the exhibit, they continued their discussion.

"You're more than just a student of history," said Cardigan. "You're also a Jew—a Jew who has neither denied nor abandoned his heritage. This much I've gathered, from your writing. Tell me—what people has been as libeled, slandered, misunderstood, misinterpreted, and derided as your own? The same Romans who branded my people ignorant, bloodthirsty barbarians called yours lazy, and biologically inferior because you refused to work one day in seven. And said that you were godless and irreverent, because your God had no images, and you refused to accept or acknowledge the gods of other peoples."

Jordan smiled. It was the smile of one who had been out-maneuvered in a friendly game of chess.

"A good point," he said. "A very good point. And very true. You've also proven an old bit of wisdom that one of my teachers loved to quote. 'Three things the wise man does not discuss—politics; religion; and a woman's age.' We've just proven ourselves unwise, since we just touched on two of the three. But, tell me—were all the accounts of Greek and Roman writers prejudiced, inaccurate, and exaggerated? Is there no truth in any of them?"

Cardigan grimaced, and thought. "Perhaps," he finally replied. "There may be some truth in what they wrote. But it would surprise me if there were very much. The writers of the Roman world—even writers in England in the last century—painted two opposing pictures of the ancient Celts. At one extreme, they were naked, grunting, blood-thirsty savages, eating raw meat, and practicing vile rites, including human sacrifice. At the other extreme, they were the prototypical 'Noble Savages,' a la Rousseau and Blake."

"And what of the middle ground, I wonder?" asked Jordan, as they meandered past the displays. "Is there one?"

"A middle ground? Yes, there is. I can recommend several books that are well-written, balanced, and give us the respect that we deserve."

"That sounds fair enough," said Jordan, noting the man's obvious indignation. "When my business here is done, we can—hmm. What's this?" he asked, as a notice on the wall caught his eye.

'LINES OF MYSTERY—POINTS OF POWER THE LEY LINES AND THE ANCIENT MYSTERIES OF BRITAIN EXPLAINED AND ILLUSTRATED BY ANDREW BARRETT AND NORA MULHOL-LAND, FOLKLORISTS & ANTIQUARIANS.'

An expression of annoyance came to the Cornishman's face as Jordan said, "'Antiquarians,' are they? I haven't heard that word for a long time. What sort of antiquated nonsense are these 'antiquarians' peddling, I wonder?"

He looked at Cardigan. "It should be amusing, even if it isn't enlightening. Shall we see what they have to say?"

"Whatever it is, I'm sure it will be nothing but pre-tentious nonsense. I've heard their sort before—including this fellow, Barrett. If you're interested, why not?"

A few minutes later, they found themselves in the room in which the talk was being held. They entered, and sat down among the audience of about fifty.

At the front of the room, Andrew Barrett and Nora Mulholland sat at a table with Mr. Richmond. Ellen Chatham sat in the front row, busily knitting like some latter-day Madame Defarge. Two projectors sat on wheeled tables nearby. A screen hung on the wall behind the speakers.

Seeing that no additional listeners were forthcoming, an uncomfortable Mr. Richmond stood up, and introduced the two speakers.

CHAPTER 12

▼

NAMES AND PLACES

"Ladies and gentlemen, welcome to the British Museum. Today we offer another in our series of lectures, 'Mysteries of the Ancient Past.' Today, we will look at the art and folklore of the ancient Celts, and at those riddles of the British landscape, the stone circles and henges. Our speakers have devoted much time to the study of that culture, and those mysteries."

After introducing Barrett and Mulholland, Richmond left the dais.

Nora spoke first. Using her own sketches, she evoked images that were reminiscent of William Blake's mysticism, and of the nineteenth-century Romantics, who saw the ancient druids as great cosmic seers, and the Celts as 'noble savages.'

She spoke for thirty minutes. From the ecstatic tone of her voice, the movement of her body, and the gleam in her eyes, one might very well believe that she personally knew the people she spoke of, and that the heroes of that lore, and the bards who sung of their mighty deeds, were her own kith and kin.

When, at last, she returned to the twentieth century, she drew a few
deep breaths, as if trying to calm down after some great excitement. Then,
she sat down, and turned the floor over to her companion.

Barrett placed his portfolio on the table in front of him, and opened it.
It held a set of maps of Britain, each one drawn on an acetate transparency.

These were no ordinary maps. One showed the territories of the Celtic
tribes of ancient Britain. Another was marked with peculiar symbols; they
represented the henges, barrows, stone circles, and burial chambers built
by Britain's most prehistoric inhabitants.

The third map showed the names and locations of several British cities
and towns. By a strange coincidence, the syllable 'ley.' or 'leigh', formed a
part of each of those place-names.

"Ladies and gentlemen," Barrett began. "for most of you, this will be
your first introduction to the culture of the ancient Celts. That race of
antiquity once held sway over much of Europe. Its members were the first
and primordial inhabitants of these British isles. Miss Mulholland has told
you something of our forebearers—our art, folklore, and religion. Now, I
should like to draw your attention to another mystery. It has existed for
many millenia, and would exist for many more, if scientific orthodoxy has
its way."

In the middle of the room, Jordan suddenly perked up. "What now?"
he thought. "Some more 'archaeological science-fiction'? Another 'pyra-
midiot'? Or more mythical 'ancient astronauts'?"

"My friends," Barrett continued, "among the ancient Celts,
three classes served as the guardians and conservators of tribal tradi-
tions, arbiters of laws, and teachers and priests of religious beliefs and
practices. They were known as the Druidh, the Filidh, and the Bardd."

The same mystical, almost rapturous attitude that had marked Nora's
presentation now characterized Andrew Barrett as he spoke. A strong,
almost ecstatic attachment to his subject was projected in his voice, and by
his motions.

It was not unnoticed by the audience. Jordan and Cardigan, both of them sensible men and keen observers of people and things, could not help but be aware of it.

"Together, they formed the priestly class of the ancient
Celts," Barrett told them. "As such, they possessed a great storehouse of knowledge. It was knowledge of a mystical nature—a knowledge which, today, would be considered occult, or paranormal. That great knowledge has, alas, been all but lost to us."

He had been speaking slowly and carefully. He now paused for a moment, to allow his words to sink into the minds of his listeners.

"Yes," he continued. "The Druids were masters of an ancient body of metaphysical lore, which they passed on to their students from generation to generation. Persecution by successive invaders—Romans, Anglo-Saxons, and Christianity—eventually led to the disappearance of the Druids, and of their secret wisdom."

A few people in the audience—including the visitor from New York and his Cornish companion—fidgeted a bit impa-tiently in their seats. They didn't know quite what to make of the man, or of his subject matter.

"Not again," thought Jordan. "Another disciple of that idiotic 'Von Daniken School' of archaeological science fiction, I'll bet. I wonder what this one's pet theory is. Megalithic computers? Prehistoric lunar observatories? Druids and 'ancient astronauts'? Whatever it is, I could use a good laugh—especially after hearing Ferguson's story, this morning."

As Barrett removed one of the maps and a felt-tipped pen from his portfolio, Llewellyn Cardigan began to sense what the man was up to. Like Jordan, he was well aware of the variety of crank theories, devised by and for the gullible, to 'explain' those riddles of Britain's landscape—its many mute and mysterious stone circles and henges. Like Jordan, he leaned forward, and waited.

"My friends, we are privileged to call a unique and extraordinary plot of ground our home. Within these British Isles lies a great power—an untapped power of wonderful psychic energy. Millenia ago, when the

Celtic tribes dwelt here in a primordial state, they lived in accord with Nature's forces. The Druids knew of those forces—they tapped into them, and used them for guidance with their prayers, rituals, and legal decisions."

Again, he paused, to let his audience absorb and appreciate what he was sharing with them. He looked at the silent, noncommittal expressions on the sea of faces in front of him. Then, he continued.

"With the supression of Druidism—first, by the Romans, then by Christianity—this wonderful knowledge was lost to us for many centuries. Here and there, a few isolated, enlighten individuals and small groups arose. They tried to rediscover and recapture some part of that lost tradition—that sacred learning.

"In their own small yet significant way, they succeeded. I would like to speak to you of two of those individuals—Katherine Maltwood, discoverer of the Glastonbury Zodiac, and Alfred Watkins, discoverer of ley lines—and of their findings."

Cardigan and Jordan felt their curiosity and skepticism aroused. So, too, was the Cornishman's anger.

"A lot of nonsense," he whispered to Jordan, with a firm shake of his head. "This should be a source of some amusement—and misinformation."

Barrett moved to one of the projectors, and placed his maps and diagrams, one at a time, on its horizontal glass plate. As the lights in the room went off, and the project-or's lamp went on, he spoke again—in a tone of absolute certainty and confidence.

"Ladies and gentlemen, observe for yourselves the incon-trovertible truth of the wisdom of the Druids, and the nature of their special, wondrous knowledge. Britain's ancient landscape and living, primordial soil hold many hundreds of megalithic tombs, barrows, stone circles, and hillforts, as well as a considerable number of henges and cursuses. Who built these great, enigmatic structures? When? How? Why? For all its vanity, and supposed knowledge, the scientific establishment has no answers."

Jordan fidgeted in his seat. Barrett had thrown down the gauntlet. Should he pick it up and throw it back? Or play it safe, and say nothing?"

Barrett's diagram stared down at them from the screen.

"This is the layout of Moel Ty Uchaf, a stone circle near Lake Bala, in Wales," he said. "An obvious indication that the Druids were highly competent architects and mathemati-cians." he added, as he moved his pen from stone to stone. "And here, we have a perfect five-pointed star—clear and absolute proof that a thousand years before the Greeks, the Druids knew how to divide a circle into five equal parts."

He wore a condescending look of triumph on his face, as he looked at the audience. Going on, he produced additional diagrams of other stone circles. Again, he drew lines from stone to stone, creating a variety of precise geometric shapes.

"My friends, I submit to you that we must acknowledge the Druids as masters of geometry, centuries before Pythagoras and Euclid."

"Do you, really?" a voice in the audience asked.

Those were the first words in English that Llewellyn Cardigan had spoken in some time.

"You've proven nothing, Mr. Barrett—except that you can draw some lines on a map. Nor have you answered your own questions. Have you any answers, I wonder? Or only your own prejudices and preconceptions, which you want to prove, even though they be groundless."

The surprise and shock on Barrett's face were equaled by the look of surprise on Jordan's face—and on the face of Ellen Chatham.

"So—he does speak English!" thought Jordan. "Why didn't he use it before?"

"Well, Mr. Barrett? What do you have to say for yourself and your 'ley lines'?" Cardigan repeated, as if he were scolding a child caught stealing cookies.

For a moment—only for a moment—Barrett and his two companions were taken aback, and at a loss for words. The rest of the audience, also, was caught off-guard by this interruption. After all, this is still England, and certain things simply weren't done.

Cardigan had spoken fighting words. Barrett could not allow his effrontery go unchallenged.

The smile on Barrett's face was the smile of one who felt sure that he was about to checkmate his opponent.

"With nearly two thousand megalithic tombs, and many hundreds of stone circles to choose from, I can offer an infinite number of alignments, to prove my claims. However, the following will serve my purpose—to highlight the wisdom of those by whom the lines were first plotted."

With those words, he placed another map on the projector.

"Please observe. Here are four diagrams of Rollright, on the Cotswolds, twenty miles northwest of Oxford. Open your mind—observe the geographical layout—its internal and external connections—the zig-zag lines, indicating the fields of electrical current discovered there."

Cardigan said nothing. He simply watched, and waited, still challenging Barrett to prove his assertions. And he smiled.

Barrett saw that smile. Well, he had another card up his sleeve, and would play it for whatever it was worth. Again, he changed maps.

A gleam came to his eye, as he anticipated putting Cardigan in his place. Again, his pen moved around the map, until it had marked and connected a series of locations. "The Glastonbury Zodiac, sir," he proclaimed, with an air of triumph. "A clear indication of the orientation of these sites, and of their purpose. See, and believe."

Cardigan simply shrugged his shoulders. Quietly, he got up, and approached Barrett. "Do you mind?" he asked, reaching for the pen.

"Not at all."

Erasing the lines drawn by Barrett, Cardigan studied the map carefully, first from one angle, then from another. Now, he took the pen, and drew some lines of his own. When he stopped, he looked at the screen, to see the enlargement of what he had drawn. Then, he spoke.

"Zodiacs? Mysticism? Lunar observatories? Nonsense, sir. If you want to know the truth, the early denizens of Glastonbury were forecasting the coming of none other than Walt Disney. You can see the proof for yourself—behold the face of Mickey Mouse, ingeniously but definitely concealed at Glastonbury Tor," he said, clearly reversing Barrett's attempted checkmate.

"What? Do you dare doubt?" he asked, in mock surprise. Erasing the image, he connected some other points. Several seconds later, a second image appeared.

"There! Let that dispel your doubts—Goofy!" he said, as the audience enjoyed a robust laugh.

"Now, do you want to know the real purpose of Glastonbury Tor? I'll show you."

Flushed with success, he drew another image, then spoke again.

"Ladies and gentlemen, allow me to tell you about the Glastonbury Bear. Obviously, it points to King Arthur, whose name is a pun on the Celtic word for 'bear'. Arthur's 'tomb' was 'found' in 1184, when the Abbey was being rebuilt—the same abbey which forms the bear's nose.

"The purpose, or task, of the 'Glastonbury Bear' should be obvious. It's on a ley line connecting the occult centers of Land's End, Avebury, and Wandlebury—a ley line designed to guide ancient astronauts. And where did these extrater-restrials come from? Why, from Ursa Major, of course—the Great Bear!"

Cardigan put the pen down. Barrett and the two women with him were dumbstruck by his audacity and blasphemy.

"Mr. Barrett, you and I have spoken of this, once or twice before," Cardigan recalled. Then, speaking as much to the audience as to Barrett, Cardigan said, "In a word, these 'ley-lines' of yours are sheer nonsense. They smack more of 'fakelore' than of folklore. I know it. You know it. And Kipling knew it, when he penned the line, 'There are nine-and-sixty ways of constructing tribal leys; And every single one of them is right'!"

CHAPTER 13

▼

THE MAIDENWELL MYSTERY

For the better part of a fortnight, the frosty air had been chilling Britain to the marrow. The sky had been filled with clouds—dense, dark, ominous clouds. They appeared to be waiting for just the right moment to dump their icy cargo on one and all, with no respect for age, race, sex, or class.

Off the coast of Cornwall, gusty winds were whipping the seas into a foam, and drove the waves against the shore with an energetic fury. The tides had long since covered the causeway leading to St. Michael's Mount. Storm warnings were in effect for all of southern England. Wind and water fought each other with a reckless abandon, as the land and its inhabitants bore the brunt of their titanic struggle.

Two of those inhabitants, Michael Craddock and Stephen Tressillian, were local police constables. They were used to such weather, and had a healthy respect for Nature's power. But their job did not allow them the luxury of staying at home, even on such a day.

With the coming of morning, their shift on duty ended. As they returned to Bodmin's police headquarters, they were looking forward to this chance to spend some time indoors, with walls and a roof between them and the elements.

"What? Back so soon?" asked Sgt. Reginald Bailey. "On such a bright, cheerful morning?"

"Not a minute too soon, if you ask me," Tressillian remarked, as he and Craddock removed their raincoats, and heated some broth. "I can't imagine any sane criminal being out in this weather. It's bloody awful out there."

"I'll say it is," a soaked Craddock readily agreed. "Not a fit night out for man or beast. Or for our bloody flesher," he added, recalling the five unsolved murders of three months earlier.

"Was that remark necessary?" Bailey snapped. "It's bad enough that we haven't been able to nab the bugger. And he's just claimed two more victims."

The three men had been involved in that case from the beginning. In fact, they were the first policemen on the scene, after the first body had been found.

"Two more?" asked Craddock. "Where, this time?"

"Right in the heart of London. One was at London Wall, the other right inside St. Paul's. Happened two days ago," Bailey told them. He paused, and finished his coffee—hoping, perhaps, that its warmth might cause his anger and frustration to evaporate.

"They happened some time late Saturday night, or early Sunday morning," he added. "From what I heard, Fergsuon and Kelly are as much in the dark now as they were when this mess first started."

"Really?" asked Tressillian, still trying to rub the cold out of his numbed hands. "Ferguson and Kelly still stumped? That news must be making headlines all around the country."

The man's surprise was understandable, and his observa-tion quite accurate. All of Britain was beginning to

believe that the Yard's dynamic duo had finally met their match. Even the unknown murderer was wondering what had happened to them.

Any speculation as to why Ferguson and Kelly had not solved the case was cut short by the opening of the front door. A young woman rushed in—was blown in, actually, by a gust of wet wind.

With a strong effort, she closed the door behind her. Her eyes darted around the room, eagerly searching for someone, or something.

Sgt. Bailey pulled up a chair, and offered it, along with some warm broth, to his soaked, worried caller. Constable Craddock took her coat, and hung it up to dry.

"Can I help you, Miss?" asked Bailey, after she had calmed down a bit.

Eagerly, the woman sat down, and accepted the proffered broth. She warmed her hands on it, then sipped it slowly. Even after she finished it, and seemed to have gotten sufficiently warmed and calm, she waited, before answering Bailey's simple question.

Her dark, nervous eyes looked around the room, then at each of the three men. Breathing deeply, she rubbed her tense face; she was not quite sure of what she should say, and how to say it.

"I'm terribly sorry, Sergeant," she finally said. "But I've just come from Maidenwell, where I had a most bizarre experience."

Under more pleasant conditions, a listener might have said that her voice was like champagne, or a flowing mountain stream.

"Bizarre? In Maidenwell? That's always been a quiet place–I can't imagine anything out-of-the-ordinary happening there. Would you care to tell me about it?"

"Want us to stay, Sergeant?" asked Craddock. "In case this needs looking into?"

"No. No, thanks. Davis and Phillips should be here soon. If it proves to be something, I can send them, or go myself." Craddock and Tressilian then left. Bailey turned to the woman again, and waited for her to tell her tale.

"In her late twenties—maybe early thirties," he thought. "A foreigner, judging from her accent. Sounds like an Aussie, perhaps. Why is she out in this weather? And what could have happened in Maidenwell?"

"My name is Janet Miller," she told him, when she regained her composure. "I'm from New Zealand, and work in London, with the New Zealand Tourist Office. Six years ago, I came to England for the first time. I spent a year in London, in University, then did some travelling, before returning home.

"In London, I became friendly with an English girl. Her name is Gwen Woodson, and she lived in St. Buryan. Gwen and I spent a month that summer touring Britain together. After I returned home we corresponded for a year. Then, she told me that she had just married, and was living with her

husband on his farm in Maidenwell."

"When did you return to England?" asked Bailey. "And how long have you been working in London?"

"Three months ago—on 17 September, to be exact. With the help of some friends, I was able to find a flat—in Croydon. I've been working at the Tourist Office since then."

After a brief pause, she went on. "Gwen and I lost contact soon after her marriage. The few letters that she wrote were very strange. She spoke of three deaths that had taken place in the area. And of periodically hearing a painful, wailing sound, in the middle of the night."

"Wailing? What sort of wailing? An animal, perhaps?"

"No. It was more like a person, in great agony," was her hushed reply. Then, "Soon afterward, her letters stopped. I wrote two or three more to her, then slowly realized that I was wasting my time.

"When I knew that I would be in England again, I wrote to her, and told her of my plans. When I arrived in London, I rang her several times, but got no answer.

"Two days ago, I left London, on what was to be a week's holiday. I decided to go to Maidenwell, and see Gwen. I wanted to learn for myself what happened to her, and why she stopped writing. I sent her a telegram, told her what train I would be on, and asked if she might meet me at the station. When I arrived, she wasn't there. I waited, but to no avail. When I rang her at home, a man answered. He was very abrupt—he said that Gwen was out, and that they didn't receive visitors."

"Is that what prompted you to come to see me?" asked Bailey. "No. Yesterday, I had the unshakeable feeling that something dreadful had happened to Gwen—that something strange and frightening was going on, in and around Maiden-well."

"What did you do, then?"

"I checked into a guest-house, here in Bodmin, then went by taxi to Maidenwell. I soon found Gwen's cottage, but several minutes passed before there was any reply. It was Gwen who opened the door. Her appearance had changed so, since I last saw her, that I could not believe my eyes.

"The pretty, vivacious girl I once knew now seemed old, worn out, and harried. She told me that she was sorry, but could not let me in. She would not even tell me why. All she would say was that the weather was bad, and it would be best if I returned to London without delay. Then I heard a man's voice urging her to shut the door, and come back inside."

Sgt. Bailey made no comment. He scratched the bridge of his nose, and grimaced slightly.

He stood up slowly. With his hands in the pockets of his tunic, he walked slowly to the front of his desk.

After a brief silence, he said, "From what you've told me, there seems to be very little that either of us can do. I hope you'll pardon my bluntness, Miss, but it appears to me that your friend wants to protect her privacy, even if it means ending old relationships. There's nothing criminal about that."

He poured a cup of tea, and gave it to her. She took it, sipped some of it. then put it down. Then, she opened her handbag, and removed an envelope with her name on it.

"This is a letter from Gwen," she told him. "I found it today, on the pillow of my bed, at the guesthouse."

Bailey looked at her quizically. "What's odd about that?" he asked.

"I was out at the time. The door was locked when I left—it was still locked, when I returned. The proprietor assured me that neither he nor his wife entered the room—and that they never allow anyone to enter the guests' rooms."

Bailey raised his eyebrows. "That is odd," he muttered. "Pray continue—what does the letter say?"

"Gwen repeats what she told me yesterday—to return to London and my job; to forget that we ever knew each other; and to make no further effort to contact her."

When she finished her story, Bailey looked at her in bewildered silence. His face was expressionless. What was he to make of it? Was the Woodson woman being held in Maidenwell against her will? Had she and her husband something to hide? Maybe so, he thought—but, then again, maybe not.

Bailey took a deep breath, and let it out with a huff.

"Let me have your friend's address, Miss Miller," he finally said. "And the name of the guest-house you're staying at. I'll drive out to Maidenwell—have a look around, ask a few questions, see what I can see."

Moved by his offer, the woman complied with his request. "Thank you," he said. "I'll look into it directly. I can't promise you more than that. But whatever happens, I'll contact you, and let you know what my inquiry reveals."

CHAPTER 14

▼

SGT. BAILEY INVESTIGATES

Sgt. Bailey looked around his office, after his fair young caller had gone. He tried to make some sense of the story that she had just told him. Was there more to it than met the eye?

"Only one way to find out—go there, and have a look for myself," he mumbled, just as Constables Davis and Philips came on duty.

"Good morning, gentlemen," he greeted them.

"Going on a holiday, Sergeant?" asked Davis.

"Indeed I am. And you, Constable, will safeguard our merry precinct-house until I return."

"Return? From where?"

"Maidenwell."

"Maidenwell? Why? Nothing ever happens there."

"Really, now? Well, let's hope that it stays that way," said Bailey, as he put on a heavy coat, and a pair of warm, waterproof boots. "I should be back in a couple of hours. A peculiar case just came in. I want to look into it."

With those words, he left the shelter of the police station, and made his way to Maidenwell. He was glad that the wind and rain had stopped by the time he reached the small hamlet. Here and there, a few scattered rays of welcome sunshine filtered through the endless expanse of clouds.

Once in Maidenwell, he soon found the house that he was looking for. In was a trim, well-tended farmhouse, with a thatched roof. Its door and window-shutters were made from sturdy English oak. The house itself was made of stone, and had a neat lawn between it and the fence that bordered the road. An acre of land, with several trees, lay behind the cottage. Chest-high shrubbery ran along three sides of the grounds, separating it from its neighbors.

Bailey looked at the brass knocker on the from door. "Recently polished. A sure sign that they take care of things," he thought.

He knocked on the door. A full two minutes passed before his knock got any reply. Then, the door opened slowly.

"Mr. Woodson?" he asked the man who now faced him across the threshold.

"Yes. My name's Woodson. Who are you? What do you want?" the man asked, defensively.

"I'm Sgt. Bailey, of the Bodmin police. We're conducting a routine search. Your home was next on my itinerary. Do you mind if I step inside for a minute? It's quite chilly out here?"

Reluctantly, Woodson stepped aside and let his unexpected visitor enter. "A routine search?" he asked, his tone softening a bit.

"That's right. And I hope it proves to be nothing more than that. It's a report of a missing person, actually. A young woman from New Zealand checked into guest-house in Bodmin three days ago; she happened to mention that she was going to visit a friend—here in Maidenwell, in fact.

She went out, early one evening, hailed a cab, and left. She hasn't been seen, or heard from, since."

Woodson lit a cigarette, and thought for a minute. "No—she hasn't been here, Sergeant," he finally said. "That much I can tell you."

"I'm sure she hasn't, Mr. Woodson," said Bailey, in friendly agreement. "But we can't afford to leave any stone unturned—routine investigation, you understand."

"Our only visitors in recent weeks have been from here in the village—and a couple from Common Moor, and some friends from Herodsfoot."

"Only local people, you say? And people you already know. You haven't seen any strangers about? Anyone needing help, or directions? Or asking anything of any of your neighbors?"

"Aside from yourself—no one," Woodson assured him.

Sgt. Bailey said nothing. He simply allowed his gaze to wander casually around the room.

The sitting room—the entire cottage, for that matter—told a lot about its owners and residents. The Woodson family had built it by hand, and had been living in it for six generations. No doubt they would live there for many generations to come.

Everything in it—everything about it—reflected a pride in craftsmanship that had all but vanished, in this age of plastics, Styrofoam, and mass-production. The furniture, curtains wooden models of old ships, even the table-lamps, were all hand-crafted.

"What about Mrs. Woodson?" asked Bailey, as his eyes finished their tour of the room.

"What about Mrs. Woodson?" a female voice repeated his question.

Bailey turned, and looked in the direction of the voice. "Mrs. Woodson?" he asked.

She stood about five feet, four or five inches in height, he estimated. Her features were sharp and angular, and her body lean. She had strong gray eyes—the first time he had ever seen that color in a woman.

"Nothing, Gwen—nothing at all," her husband was quick to reply. "Something—or someone—seems to have gotten lost, or gone astray. The Sergeant wants to know if we've seen any strangers about, the past few days."

"Strangers? Here in Maidenwell?"

"Yes, ma'am. A young girl from New Zealand—been missing for three days. Said she was coming out here to visit a friend. Unfortunately, she didn't tell anyone the name and address of the people she was planning to visit. Anyway, I'm sorry if I disturbed you—duty, you understand."

Bailey turned to leave. "Thanks for your time, Mr. Woodson," he said, as he placed a hand on the doorknob. "If either of you should hear or see anything, would you please ring me? Well, good day to you."

CHAPTER 15

▼

CLOVIS LOVINGTON HOBBS

An hour later, Sgt. Bailey was sitting in his office. He was leaning slightly back, apparently lost in thought. The fingers of his left hand were drumming slowly on the arm of his chair.

Like it or not, he now had to ring Janet Miller, and tell her the simple truth. He had seen, heard, and learned nothing to hint that anything unlawful was going on in the Woodson home.

Was Mrs. Woodson being held there against her will? Had she been beaten or abused in any way? He couldn't say.

Miss Miller would have to accept the disappointing news—that he learned nothing, in his one visit to the Woodson home, to justify any action by the police.

After a brief reflection, he reached for the phone, rang Miss Miller, and told her of his call on the Woodson's.

"What would you advise?" the anxious woman asked.

Bailey thought for a moment. "I saw nothing that warrants a police investigation," he told her. "The only suspicious thing is that both husband and wife denied that they had seen or met any strangers—and, more particularly, that they had seen or heard of anyone from New Zealand."

"They're lying, Sergeant," she replied. "I don't know why, but they're lying. They must be hiding something, if they told you that. They must be. I can think of no other explanation. But what are we to do about it?"

"For the present, Miss Miller, the thing not to do is panic, or jump to any hasty conclusions," he told her. "We'll keep our eyes and ears open. I'll let you know if and when we learn anything. As things look now, there's very little else I can do."

Their brief conversation ended on that note. Having seen and heard nothing to warrant police interference, Sgt. Bailey certainly could not accuse the Woodson's of any wrong-doing, or of any sort of mischief.

Returning the phone to its cradle, Bailey wondered about Miss Miller, and her agitated frame of mind. He finally concluded that she had simply overreacted to Mrs. Woodson's desire to terminate their friendship, and to her changed appearance. He believed that she should follow Mrs. Woodson's advice—return to London and her job, and treat their friendship as a thing of the past. He had wanted to tell her as much, over the phone. But he didn't believe that she would have listened to him, if he had.

Not long after speaking with Bailey, Janet Miller was carrying her two small suitcases, and on her way to the Bodmin railway station. Several hours later, she was back in her Croydon flat.

She heated up a cup of coffee, and a bowl of lentil soup, as she sought to calm herself down. She drank both slowly, as she tried to sort out her thoughts, and decide what to do next.

She was convinced that something was dreadfully amiss in the Woodson household. She had come to believe that Gwen Woodson was staying in Maidenwell against her will, and that it was not of her own volition that she had chosen to terminate their friendship.

he had been entertaining these thoughts for the past week. The more she thought them, the more she convinced herself that all was not right, in that cottage in Maidenwell.

Having convinced herself of this, she could not understand why Sgt. Bailey did not agree with her. Why had he learned nothing, in his visit to Maidenwell?

The answers—her own answers, the ones that she wanted to hear, and to believe—began to form in her distressed mind, as she poured and drank another cup of coffee.

Obviously, Bailey did not believe her. He had treated her like a little child, and had gone to Maidenwell merely to humor her.

That he found nothing to support her suspicions served only to increase them. Either Sgt. Bailey did not know his business, she told herself, or James Woodson was a masterful liar.

Either way, she was not going to sit still. She was not yet certain as to what she would do, or how she might do it, but she was determined to do something.

The following morning, after a troubled night's sleep, Janet Miller left her flat with a definite purpose in mind. Since Sgt. Bailey could not help her, she would get assist-ance elsewhere—she would go to London, and enlist the aid of Scotland Yard.

In London, she went directly to Scotland Yard. Entering the tall building on Victoria Street, she approached the information desk.

"What if they don't believe me?" she suddenly wondered. "What if they think that I'm daft, and refuse to help? It doesn't matter—Gwen is in trouble. I must do what I can, to help her."

"Yes, Miss?" the receptionist asked her.

"I want to report a missing person. I believe she may have been kidnapped—or is being detained somewhere against her will."

Looking at the constable on duty, the receptionist asked,

"That's Insp. Hobbs' department, isn't it?"

The man nodded. The woman then picked up the phone, and dialed a number. "Front desk, Inspector. A case for you—report of a missing person, possible kidnapping."

She put the phone down, then asked the nervous caller, "Have you any identification, Miss? Thank you. Here's your visitor's pass. The lift is midway down the corridor, on your left. Insp. Hobbs' office is Number 509."

Miss Miller hastily mumbled a 'thank you,' took the pass, and hurriedly made her way to Room 509. Once there, she knocked on the door. A voice from within bade her enter. What she saw surprised her almost as much as had her experience in Maidenell.

The man didn't fit her image of a police detective. He reminded her of Sir Percy Blakeny—thin, carefully groomed, more suited to Ascot or a drawing room than to the harsh world of police work.

But Clovis Lovington Hobbs was every inch a detective. And he had a reputation for patience, compassion, and chivalry—all, in fact, that Miss Miller was looking for.

He made her welcome, and listened to her tale. She told him everything—including her amazement at the fact that Bailey's brief visit to Maidenwell had failed to substanti-ate her fears.

"I'm at my wits' end, Inspector," she concluded. "I'm certain that something dreadful has happened to Gwen, and that she's not free to act for herself. The police in Bodmin were of no help at all—none whatsoever. I've come here in—well, in desperation. I don't know where else to turn, or what to do."

Hobbs readjusted his eyeglasses. "Yes, I daresay you have," he said, after a brief, thoughtful silence. "And your story presents as much a problem for me as it does for you."

"A problem? Why?"

"Our jurisdiction is limited to Greater London. We rarely get involved in cases around the country, unless our help is sought by the local police. Otherwise, we respect their jurisdiction, and their judgement and abilities."

He paused. Then, "Miss Miller, if I can help you in any way, you have my word that I shall. But if all fairness, I must tell you that I'm inclined to agree with Sgt. Bailey."

She flushed with anger and resentment. "I should have known better. I'm sorry if I've wasted your time."

She rose to leave. "I suppose that I must act on my own. Gwen may be in serious danger, but the police refuse to do anything. That seems typically English. Sit back—do nothing—don't make waves—simply wait until some disaster falls into your laps. Thank God I'm not English!"

"Quite the contrary, Miss Miller," Hobbs was quick to reply. "From what you've told Sgt. Bailey and myself, you do have one very human, trait."

"Do I really? And what might that be?"

"You're unwilling and unable to see and accept the obvious. Mrs. Woodson wishes to protect her privacy, even if it means severing past relationships. Whatever her reasons—even if it is merely an eccentricity—she wants to do it. There is nothing criminal in that. And because there is not, I can do nothing to help you."

Now, both of them were annoyed and exasperated.

"Miss Miller," he finally said, "from what you've told me, I see no evidence of any wrong-doing—none whatsoever. Your pride has been wounded. Perhaps something has happened to Mrs. Woodson—something un-known to us—which prompted her to dissolve her friendship with you. If so, it might explain the change that you perceived in her appearance."

"Then you do believe me, Inspector?" she asked—almost pleaded, as if she were drowning, and reaching for a floating spar.

"I don't know if I believe you," he said. "But I don't disbelieve you. Only time, and a possible inquiry, can tell us if your fears have substance or not."

"I can't, and won't, promise any miracles," he added, after a moment's pause. "Whatever else you may have heard about Scotland Yard, we are human. There are limits as to what we can do. As soon as those limits allow, I will look into this case. Whether that satisfies you or not, it will have to suffice."

"Yes, I suppose it must," she said. "And if you do learn anything—anything, no matter what it is—you will let me know, won't you?"

"Most assuredly, Miss Miller. You can rely on it," he promised her. With that assurance, she turned and left.

A perplexed Clovis Hobbs now stood in the silence of professional sanctuary. He didn't know quite what to say or think about Miss Miller and her problem.

His puzzlement lasted for but a few short minutes. Then, he concluded that her pride had been hurt; she simply did not want to accept the fact that a friendship had ended. Her problem was obviously trivial and mundane—so much so, he decided, that it did not exist outside her distraught imagination. Obviously.

With that, he chose to take a brief recess from his work. He had to regain his composure, after that annoying waste of his valuable time. He left his office, and walked down the corridor, when he met Kelly emerging from the Yard's library.

CHAPTER 16

▼

THE DREAM

A frosty darkness had already covered England when Jordan and Cardigan returned to Victoria Street. Ferguson and Kelly were just coming off duty, after another long, frus-trating day. And Jordan was beginning to feel the fatigue—the jet lag, and two days without sleep, were now catching up with him.

"Well, I see that you found your way back here without any difficulty," Kelly greeted them. His voice lacked the zest and buoyancy that were present, earlier that day.

"Yes, we did," said Jordan. "It proved to be an inter-esting afternoon. We'll have to tell you about it. That is, if the jetlag doesn't do me in," he added, as he tried to rub the fatigue from his face.

"No cause for alarm, Professor," Kelly assured him. "Cardigan can spend the night with me, at my flat. No reason for him to return to St. Ives tonight. It will also give us a chance to talk about his gift."

"Now, don't get carried away, Kelly," Ferguson advised him, in a friendly tone.

"Quite frankly, I would like to get carried away, once in a while—away from the pressures, the tension, the damned frustration—and our public image. Can I expect the same of you?"

"What do you mean by that? Of course you can."

"I seem to recall that after that case at Tintagel, you stayed up to the wee hours of the morning, listening to Jordan's stories. So, please remember—business before pleasure. At least, until this affair is settled."

With that, they parted company. John Kelly took Cardigan home with him, to spend the evening discussing ancient Celtic lore, and the Cornishman's gift. And Jordan returned with Ferguson, to the latter's home on Kenneth Crescent.

"So the old boy does speak English?" said a surprised Ferguson, after Jordan had told him how he had spent the afternoon. "He speaks English, and from what you tell me, he's not the sort to tolerate any sort of nonsense."

"That's right. And he's not afraid to speak his mind, openly and candidly. If nothing else, it proves one thing—he'd be a failure in politics."

Ferguson nodded. Then, changing the subject, he said, "One of our colleagues told us a curious story today. It involves a missing person."

"A missing person? Do you suspect foul play?"

"An interesting possibility. I hadn't thought of it—not consciously, that is. I've been too preoccupied. But it is worth considering."

A faint light came to his tired, troubled eyes. "I'll sleep on it tonight," he said. "If it's true, I'll give you honourable mention when we nab the culprit." With that, they put aside all thoughts of crime, and went into the house.

"My word—don't we look chipper this evening," Peggy Ferguson greeted them.

"You know, you really must meet my wife, Naomi," said Jordan.

"The two of you already have at least one thing in common."

"Do we?" Peggy asked.

"Yes. You both have husbands who are married as much to their professions as to their wives."

"In that case, if we were to sue our husbands for divorce, we might blame that dedication—for alienation of affections."

She laughed a healthy, intoxicating laugh. It was an infectious laugh, which couldn't fail to affect the two men.

"By the way, you never really told us about your wife," she added. "She must be a special woman, to put up with the demands of your work."

"Yes, she is. She's a social worker—working mainly with the elderly. She knows what it's like to be deeply involved in one's work. And it's been a strain on both of us, ever since we got married," he told her.

"Have you ever regretted it? Your choice of profession, I mean," Ferguson asked him.

"Yes and no. I regret the strains on my family, and the fact that it takes me away from them so often. But I really can't imagine myself doing anything else. And I've seen, done, and learned things that I otherwise would not have. So, it's a standoff of sorts," he said, as they sat down to eat.

Soon afterward, Jordan went to bed. Even before his head hit the pillow, he fell into a deep sleep. His breathing soon became slow and regular. Then, he began to dream—blurred, fleeting images at first, with no real meaning. The hazy images raced before his mind's eye. When they stopped, all became a deep and impenetrable blank. Soon, he reached a deep level of unconsciousness, and began to dream—a specific dream, with a specific purpose.

As the shadows receded, he saw a rough-hewn stone pillar. It stood as high as a man's chest. On each of its rugged, uneven sides was a weathered human figure.

A group of people stood in the background. All wore long linen robes, and strange, frightening medallions, and were chanting in low tones. Two men and two women stood next to the stone, and poured a few drops of some thick liquid onto it.

As if animated by some strange power, the pillar assumed a life of its own. Very faintly, it began to expand and contract.

This negligible movement soon became stronger. As if absorbing some awful energy from the celebrants, and from their ritual, the stone began to pulsate, and emit long, low, horrid moans.

In his mind's eye, the sleeper watched in hypnotized wonder, as the top of the stone divided into two, then into four, and then became one again.

Each of its four faceless guardians now placed a wreath of mistletoe on this most other-worldly pillar. Then, they anointed the wreaths and the stone with some strange-scented oil.

A wicker basket containing a human head and entrails was now placed atop the wreaths, and a torch applied to them. The foul flames rose up, and the horrid stench assailed the nostrils of the worshippers.

As it did, the sleeper's attention now saw something else. Dark, purplish blood began to ooze from the sides of the pillar.

Four times before had he dreamed a similar dream. But not until now had he seen such vivid, horrifying details. He had searched for possible meanings to this recurring nightmare, but to no avail.

Eliezer Jordan slept, and dreamed to its end his dark, grim dream. When that welcome end finally came, he shuddered involuntarily. Turning over, he buried himself under the covers, as if trying to turn away from that awful vision, and hide from its possible return.

His breathing now became lighter. He awoke twice during that long, cold night—very briefly. Reassuring himself of where he was, and why he was there, he slept peacefully until morning.

CHAPTER 17

▼

WITH MALCOLM MORGAN

The morning following Cardigan's effrontery at the British Museum, Andrew Barrett and his female companions returned to Paddington Station. They were talking quietly in the buffet car as the train arrived in Plymouth.

"Cardigan's insult can't go unanswered, Andrew. It mustn't!" Ellen Chatham insisted, as she went on with her ever-present knitting.

Barrett, who had borne the brunt of Cardigan's ridicule, was sitting back in his seat. He looked at his angry companion.

"No, Ellen, it certainly mustn't" he agreed. "It will be answered, if I have anything to say about it."

Others were now entering the buffet car. Knowing the value of discretion, Barrett dropped the subject for the time being.

The train finally reached Penzance, and the end of its run. Passengers and crew disembarked, and went their separate ways. For the three 'keepers of the ley lines', the journey was not yet over. A member of their circle was waiting with a car, to drive them to St. Buryan.

Afternoon gave way to evening, and a wintry darkness descended upon St. Buryan. Barrett put on a sheepskin coat, and a woolen cap and muffler, and went to call on Malcolm Morgan.

Morgan was a strong, agile man. Like Barrett, he was born and bred in Cornwall—in St. Buryan, and baptized in the local church. Both had a thorough knowledge of local history, geography, and tradition. And they shared an interest in, and devotion to, the old ways—an interest and devotion that filled and guided their lives.

"Come in, Andrew," Alice Morgan greeted him. "Malcolm's been looking forward to seeing you this evening."

"Any special reason?"

"Perhaps," was her cryptic reply.

The local vicar was just leaving when Barrett and Alice Morgan and entered the sitting room. Malcolm was standing there, arms folded, a scowl clouding his rugged features.

"Seeking converts again?" Barrett correctly assumed.

Morgan grunted, and nodded. "The old fool still refuses to believe that he'll find no converts here."

"Nor in any of a few dozen others we can take him to," Barrett added, confidently. The tone of his voice contrasted most cheerfully with the mood that he had been in, earlier that day.

"Alice tells me that you wanted to see me," said Morgan, as he lit his pipe.

"Yes, I do," said Barrett. But I need something to calm my nerves, first—I always do, after a session with a preacher."

A few minutes later, both men and the woman were seated around a low, wooden table. "How did your talk at the Museum go, Andrew?" Morgan asked him. "Did anyone express an interest in your topic? Or in joining our Circle?"

"Yes, Malcolm. One person was interested," was Barrett replied. "But it wasn't exactly what we had hoped for. In fact, it was quite the opposite—a most antagonistic interest, if you must know."

He took a hearty drink of ale, then continued. "It would be all too easy to say that I should have sensed something, as soon as we encountered Richmond's disrespectful attitude," he began.

"Richmond? Who is he?" asked Morgan.

"The Museum's Assistant Curator of Celtic and Anglo-Saxon art. Assistant curator, mind you. Apparently we didn't merit the attention of the Curator," said Andrew, with a sneer.

Morgan said nothing. He simply sat there, and listened quietly to Andrew's story. "Your afternoon certainly wasn't dull," he said, when his friend was through. "I'll say that much for it."

He sympathized with his friend's anger and discomfort. He would probably have felt the same, were he in Barrett's place. He had already had several similar confrontations with the clergy since his conversion to paganism, all far less pleasant than this one in the British Museum.

"Dull, Malcolm? No, it wasn't dull—I can say that much for it. It remains to be seen what is to be done about it—what can be done about it," said Barrett, as he got up, and nervously paced the room.

"We can invite him to take part in one of our rituals," Morgan casually suggested. "Perhaps as the guest of honour at a sacrifice at the Cairn."

"Quite frankly, I like the idea—for him, and for Richmond. I'd like to teach them both a lesson for their irreverence." "You're hungry for revenge, I see. Well, here's something else to think about. I have some news for you."

Barrett looked at his friend. "News? What sort of news?"

"Ever hear of a man called Jordan?"

"Jordan? No. Who is he?"

"An American archaeologist. Made a name for himself digging in the Middle East, I heard."

"So? What's that have to do with us? Is he planning to dig in Britain? Or join our Circle?"

"I hardly think so, Andrew. He's a Jew—very little chance of him turning to paganism, or of condoning our particular cultic practices."

"So why mention him?"

A worried expression came to the druid's face. He refilled and relit his pipe, then said, "Do you remember that affair at Tintagel, two years ago?"

"Of course. But how does it tie in with this fellow? And what does he have to do with us?"

"Thus far, nothing. And I want to keep it that way. His presence in England, now, is no coincidence. I've heard things about him, from friends here in England, and on the continent. I've heard similar things far too often to discount them as idle gossip."

"To answer your questions," he said, after a brief pause, "a well-placed friend later told me that it was he, not the police, who solved that case. He managed to enter a druidic circle—one of the most secret—and then got word to the police."

Barrett began to see his friend's point, but did not share his concern. "Aren't you overreacting, Malcolm?"

Morgan shook his head.

"He got lucky," said Barrett. "That's all."

"The two men at the Yard who worked on that case are now leading the search for us. One of them met Jordan at Gatwick yesterday morning," Morgan told him.

"Which would mean that he's not here merely for the scenery," Barrett correctly guessed.

"He most certainly isn't," Morgan readily agreed. "And if the stories about him are true, and my suspicions are correct, we have to be careful. He may cross our path, before long."

"What stories?"

"He's supposed to have studied the mystical lore of the Jews—the Qabbalah, they call it. It's not nearly as old as our own, but it's said to be quite potent. He's said to have mastered it, and to be able to do things beyond human ability and understanding."

"Well, Malcolm," said Barrett, after a moment's thought, "if what you say is true, it might be interesting to see what would happen if he does come our way."

"Why this sudden bravado, Andrew?" asked Alice, speaking for the first time. "You admit that you know nothing about him. Why this sudden eagerness to meet him?"

"Perhaps it's the challenge of an encounter between two opposing creeds. Perhaps I'm still smarting, after the sting of Cardigan's effrontery, yesterday."

Morgan didn't share his friend's attitude. He didn't lack self-confidence, nor was he wanting in his devotion to the ancient ways. As for challenges, and conflicting outlooks, he had met quite a few, and had held his own fairly well each time. He was no coward as far as that, or anything else, was concerned.

He was no fool, either. He was practical and sensible. He knew when conditions called for bold, direct action, and when they called for cunning or restraint.

"Now, Andrew, I think that we should take care. We've managed to elude the police until now. I want to keep it that way. No need to let wounded pride become the rope by which they find and hang us."

"I suppose you're right," Barrett finally agreed. "'Act in haste, repent at leisure.' Is that it?"

"Exactly. The safety and survival of our circle, and our people, are at stake."

Morgan now stood up, and refilled their mugs. In an effort to lighten the serious mood, he put a rectangular board, and a pad and pen, on the table.

"This might interest you, Andrew," he said. "It's another board-game I've been working on. It's based on the legend of Bran."

"Yes, it does. And it's quite appropriate, in view of the fact that his head was cut off, and buried on Ludgate Hill."

"Yes, it is, isn't it? I wonder if the police will ever see a connection between that, and the two killings last week-end."

"I doubt it," said Barrett, with a laugh. Then, noting the clock on the wall, he said, "I'd best be leaving, now. It's getting late, and I've had two busy days."

"Very well," said Morgan, as he emptied his pipe into the fireplace. "By the way, Andrew, don't forget that we're going to Redruth, Sunday morning."

Barrett paused for a minute, his hand on the door-knob. "Redruth?" he asked. What with his anger after his encounter with Cardigan, he had temporarily forgotten all about it.

"Redruth? Oh, yes—of course. I only hope that it will be worth the effort, and bear some fruit."

"So do I," the druid agreed. "But if it can bring the druidic circles one step closer to unity and harmony, it will be worth the effort." With those words, the two men parted company.

They put aside all thoughts of ritual killings, the police, and students of the Kabbalah. They were discrete men, and in their discretion lay their safety. There was little need to be fearful or distraught, for the ancient ones of Albion were on their side.

CHAPTER 18

▼

GOING TO BODMIN

The sleeping figure slowly began to return to conscious-ness. First one muscle moved, and then another. At last, he came to life.

He sat up. With some effort, he rubbed the fatigue from his face. He looked—and felt—like one who had been anesthetized, and had not yet overcome the effect.

"Hmm," Jordan muttered, as he slid his feet to the floor, and inched himself out of bed. "I haven't slept so long, or so deeply, in a long time. And that dream!" He grimaced, recalling it as he filled the bathroom sink with cold water, and began to wash.

"That was some frightful dream. Incubation?" he asked himself, as he began to shave. "An indication of things to come?"

That possibility gave him food for thought.

"It may well be. But what of it? Well, I won't find the answer, standing here—I have a train to catch. Perhaps part of the answer is in Bodmin."

He was now fully awake. With his characteristic speed and efficiency, he got dressed, and tossed a few basic necessities into his tote bag. He went to the kitchen for a quick snack, and found a note waiting for him on the table. It was written in a woman's hand.

"Coffee and scones waiting on stove," it said. "Eggs in fridge—help yourself. Peggy."

Underneath, her husband added, "Ring me before you leave. Would like to know your whereabouts in case of trouble."

A smile came to his face as he read the note, put it in his pocket, then took the biscuits from the stove. He appreci-ated his friend's request. After all, this was Ferguson's case, and they were working on it together, albeit from different perspectives.

Now, he picked up the phone, and rang his friend at work. "I'm just about to leave," he told Ferguson. "It's 8:40—I want to catch the 10:05 to Liskeard. Yes, I'll let you know the name of the guesthouse I'll be staying at, and where I expect to go. I understand. I'll keep you posted. Good-bye."

Jordan hung up, then put on his parka, gloves, and woolen cap and scarf. Leaving the house, he went by underground to Paddington Station. Once there, he checked the huge information board for the track-number of his train. Then, walking to the correct gate, he stood there silently, and immersed himself in thought.

All around him were the noise, activity, and year-end bustle of a busy metropolis. But he was oblivious to all of it.

With a single-mindedness that came easy to him, he shut himself off to his surroundings, and focused his attention on the problem at hand. He thought of the epidemic of horrible murders—of the anger and sorrow of the victims' families, and of the frustration and helplessness of the police. Recalling the two reports that Ferguson had shown him, he began to wonder about the acts themselves—the thoughts and feelings of the murderer, and of the victims, during the last few seconds preceding death.

What could he assume from what Ferguson had told him? That a homicidal madman was on the loose? Homicidal—yes; that much seemed certain.

Mad? Who could say? Jordan was no psychiatrist, but life had taught him that a lack of moral scruples did not neces-sarily constitute insanity. But sane or mad, a killer was on the loose, and had to be stopped.

Who was this anonymous, merciless adversary, who mutilated his vic-tims so carefully? Whoever he was, whatever his motives, he was still free—free to continue his murderous mischief when and where he pleased. And he, Eliezer Jordan, had been asked by his friend, Sean Ferguson, to come to England, to use his mystical knowledge in the effort to find the culprit.

His reverie was soon brought to a sharp halt. A voice on a loudspeaker announced that his train was now boarding passengers. Showing his ticket to the guard, he went through the gate, and boarded the train. In a matter of minutes, he was on his way.

Jordan had quite a job ahead of him. He couldn't rely on anyone for help, except Ferguson and Kelly. The local police were sure to resent any interference—especially from a civilian. But he often had to work alone on his cases—it was something that he had come to take for granted.

"What of the families of the victims?" he wondered. "Would any of them be willing to talk to me? Quite honestly, I couldn't blame them if they weren't."

With a shrug of his shoulders, he resigned himself to a difficult, dan-gerous task.

When, at last, he heard his destination announced, he got up, and took his things. Two minutes later, the train arrived at Liskeard, and he disem-barked.

The sun had already come out from behind the clouds by the time Jordan stepped onto the platform at Liskeard. It lit up the sky with a pale silvery hue. Jordan took only passing notice of it—his mind was focused on more serious matters.

He wasted no time. Getting a car at a local rental agency, he drove to a guesthouse and checked in. Then, he emptied his two small bags, and arranged their contents on the bed.

He looked at the large note-pad on which he had written the

basic data of each murder. Next to it were two maps—one, a road map of Cornwall and Devon, had various sites and attractions marked, and had been provided by the car-hire agency; the other was a large ordinance map that he had borrowed from Ferguson.

And there was his 'tool-kit'—a blue terry-cloth robe; a brown woolen skull-cap, knitted by one of his daughters; a beige woolen prayer-shawl, a hand-made gift from his wife; a cassette-player; and two cassettes with music that he had chosen and recorded for his specific, rather unconventional purpose.

Alone among students of the Kabbalah, he used an outside aid—in his case, music—to induce mystical trances. He smiled as he looked at it, and thought of this.

"These things aren't normally associated with criminal investigations. Then again, neither is the Kabbalah," he mused, with a smile.

He looked at his watch—it was two-thirty. There were still about two hours of daylight left. Taking only his pad and a map, he drove to Bodmin, where the first murder had occurred, three months earlier.

Once there, he parked the car, and sat for a few minutes. He studied the map, and the notes that he had made, the previous morning, reviewing them out loud.

"Let me see. Five murders in September, five in October, two in December. Six days between the first two and the next three. Nothing for five weeks, then two, and two more ten days later. I wonder if the time between the killings might mean anything," he thought, as he recalled the role of numerology in mysticism. "Could be, but I better not jump to any hasty conclusions," he wisely cautioned himself.

It was 2:42 when he put his pad and map aside, and got out of the car. He took note of the sights and sounds around him. He felt unusually invigorated by the cold, crisp air, as he walked towards the churchyard, where the first body had been found.

"Found there, but believed to have been killed elsewhere," he reminded himself, recalling Ferguson's report. Three-and-a-half months had passed since then. What could Jordan possibly hope to find, or do, now?

The poor victim had been buried, and all signs of the gruesome deed were gone. Now, her family and friends had to live with their grief and their nightmares, and with a frustrated hatred of the unknown cause of their sorrow.

He walked briskly towards his destination. He paused for just a moment, as his hand rested on the latch of the graveyard gate. Just then, he had a premonition of just what he might be facing a sensation that Death itself was lurking nearby.

He shook his head, in an effort to free himself of any fears. Then, he opened the gate, and entered. He walked slowly along until he found what he was looking for-the grave over which the murdered girl's body had been placed.

Why had her killer left her there? A perverted whim? Or some dark, diabolical reason?

He tried to read the inscription that time and the elements had already begun to erode. He read that faded memorial, and wondered about the life and death of the one whose stone it was. Naught but that time-worn tombstone, and a hole in the ground for that desiccated clay, testified that a living being had once passed this way. Jordan made a mental note of the inscription, then stood up.

Attracted by a light in the window, he approached the church, and entered. Walking through the old stone structure, he knocked on a sturdy pine door. In response to a voice within, he opened it, and entered.

CHAPTER 19

▼

A GRUESOME FIND

Eliezer Jordan had seen, done, and learned many things in his lifetime. He had traveled widely, and encountered an interesting assortment of people, customs, and experiences. But none of that prepared him for the sight that greeted him when he entered the vicar's study.

Seated in a chair was the body of a man in his late fifties. His hands and feet had only recently been amputated. An expression of horror was indelibly etched on his face. On a table near the window was a hand-woven straw basket. In it lay a wreath of mistletoe. In the middle of the wreath were the man's severed parts. A sweet-smelling ointment had been sprinkled over the basket's gruesome contents.

Jordan stood there, his hand firmly gripping the doorknob. His strong face wore a look of shock. For what seemed an eternity, no one in the room moved, or said a word. The uncomfortable silence was broken by Sgt. Reginald Bailey of the Bodmin police.

"Yes? Can I help you?" he asked.

Jordan said and did nothing. It took a few minutes, and a strong effort on his part, to overcome his initial shock, and find his voice.

"I hope so, Sergeant," he finally said. "I was hoping to speak with the vicar. But I seem to have come at an awkward moment." "So it would seem," Bailey agreed. "As you can see, we have an important matter to deal with. If you'll excuse us, your talk with him will have to wait."

Sgt. Bailey returned to his unpleasant task. Two ambulance attendants carefully removed the body, and took it to the hospital, where the autopsy would be performed. Two con-stables removed the basket, with its gruesome contents, and followed them.

Bailey placed a reassuring hand on the pastor's arm. "We'll get the bugger who did this," he said. "Sooner or later, he's bound to slip up. He's bound to," he repeated, more as a wish than a certainty. "I'll be back as soon as I can, to continue the investigation. And let me know if I can help you in any way."

The poor clergyman nodded listlessly. It would take some time for his shock to subside—the shock of what he had seen, of his discovery of the body, the fear that it was starting again.

He gazed around the room, then sat down in chair near the window. As he sat there, thinking of the horror of what he had seen, the door of the study opened, and a stranger entered. As if prompted by some sixth sense, Mr. Thomson turned, and looked in numbed silence at his unexpected visitor.

A strange aura surrounded the newcomer—an aura of strength and mystery. Thomson sensed it, even though he didn't fully understand it.

"Excuse me if I don't get up," he said, almost in a whisper. "You see, there's been a murder—a murder, and I found the body." His voice trailed off.

"I know," said the stranger. "And I want to find the mur-derer before he kills again."

After a brief silence, the vicar spoke again. "I'm sorry—do come in. Sit down." He nodded towards a chair. With an obvious effort, he tried to regain his composure.

The newcomer took off his coat, sat down, and faced the priest.

"Are you a policeman? You're certainly not English," said Thomson, in an unsteady voice.

"My name is Eliezer Jordan. I'm neither English nor a policeman, but I am working with Scotland Yard. Are you well, sir?"

The vicar looked at his mysterious visitor, but said nothing. His face wore an expression of fear, fatigue, and anger, because of what he had seen.

"Can you tell me what happened?" asked the stranger.

"A murder has been committed, sir. Here, in God's holy sanctuary! The honour of God has been stained by this wicked deed."

"All creation is God's sanctuary," said his visitor. "Any wicked deed, anywhere, defiles His holy name. But tell me of this one."

He was very much aware of the shock that the vicar had suffered. He did not want to add to the strain, but he was in no mood to let matters rest.

Breathing slowly and deeply, Mr. Thomson recalled those earlier murders for Jordan. He remembered them—and other things, of an equally unpleasant nature, that he had read and heard as a boy. He recalled things that he had seen and heard around the countryside—things of a strange nature—things that were best left alone, untouched and undisturbed. Then, his thoughts returned to his visitor.

Fortified slightly by the solitude, the church, and his attentive visitor, the vicar was more nearly himself.

"I'm afraid that the murders of three months ago may have begun anew," he began. "I had just paid a visit to one of my parishioners. When I returned, I found the body, sitting there. Albert Stedman was a horticulturist. His specialty was roses, you know. There was hardly a thing about roses that he didn't know."

Thomson paused. Going to his desk, he poured a glass of water and drank it slowly and deeply. That simple act seemed to help him regain some of his composure.

"He was a member of my church until about six years ago. When I asked him why he stopped coming, he said that he had found something else to occupy his time." His voice trailed off.

"Did he tell you what it was?"

"No. He simply replied that he had found something more interesting and rewarding, to occupy his time and energy. Yes, those were his words— 'more interesting and rewarding.'"

"And he never mentioned what it was?" Jordan asked.

The vicar frowned, rubbing his chin while staring at the American. Jordan read a reluctance to speak, in the vicar's face. Thomson studied the man, as if trying to pierce his aura.

Then, "No, he didn't say." he replied. "But I had some suspicions—suspicions I was never able to prove. There are places in England where the old ways still survive. They may be in small, harmless ways, but here and there some dark and hidden evil is still lurking, waiting for the chance to reach out and claim a victim."

"Like Albert Stedman?"

"Yes—like him. And, if my fears are well-founded, like those others, three months ago. And I must share the guilt for those deaths. I should have worked harder to bring those people back to God."

"A man will choose his own path, God or no God. We can only hope that the path chosen is one of life, and of enlightenment," said Jordan.

The pastor thought for a minute. "Yes, I suppose so," he said, in a tone of some resignation. "Even still, I can't help feeling that I ought to have done something to prevent this."

"Either way, Mr. Thompson, we can't bring back the dead. But we can try to find the killer—to prevent further deaths, and see justice done. Will you help me?"

The vicar nodded. "Yes. What can I do? What do you want to know?"

"Whatever you can tell me about Albert Stedman, and any of the earlier victims."

CHAPTER 20

▼

MR. HOBBS' DILEMMA

John Kelly's face wore a look of frustration, fatigue, and annoyance as he emerged from the Yard's library. This was his third visit there in as many weeks. He had just spent three hours there, pouring patiently over the records of known murderers, and of cases involving serial killings.

Carefully, he had checked all the data. He examined, compared, and contrasted. He had not found the hoped-for perspective—no new insight or clue to help him in this frustrating case.

Kelly's mood was as gray and downcast as the weather. His mood was foul as he left the library and headed for his office. He didn't respond very warmly when he heard his name called, in a rather hearty manner, by a voice down the corridor.

"I say, Kelly," the caller hailed him. "You're looking rather down this morning. Is something amiss?"

Kelly's annoyance was all too obvious as he came to a halt. With a scowl on his face, he turned around, and saw Clovis Hobbs approaching.

"Amiss? Hmph! Of course something is amiss!" he snapped. "There have been two more murders—in case you haven't heard."

Hobbs wore a look of genuine distress on his face. "Well, Kelly, what are we going to do about it?" he asked, as they walked to Kelly's office.

"Do? 'We?' What, and whom, did you have in mind?" Kelly wondered.

"I was thinking of Singh, Kassim, and myself, of course. Oh, I know that this case officially belongs to you and Ferguson, but what's to prevent the three of us from helping you?"

"Very little, I should say," said Kelly, as they reached his office. He opened the door and went in, followed by Hobbs. "Unless, of course, you have a case of your own to work on."

Ferguson looked over as Kelly sat down at his desk. The latter tilted his seat back, and withdrew into the privacy of his own thoughts.

Without waiting for an invitation from either Ferguson or Kelly, Hobbs took an empty seat. He leaned forward, eager for a reply from Kelly.

Ferguson was standing by the window. He observed his two colleagues with a trace of amusement. "Are you two up to something?" he asked. "Can anyone play?"

Kelly shifted his weight ever so slightly. Turning his head a bit, he said, "Hobbs here would like to know if any-thing 'is amiss.' And if he, Singh, and Kassim might help us in some way."

Ferguson raised his eyebrows, and pouted. "What could be amiss, my dear Hobbs? It's business as usual here."

Frustrated, Hobbs replied, "There were two strange murders last week-end. And you're no closer to a solution than you were four months ago, when it all began."

Kelly scowled. "Have you no cases of your own to worry about?" he wondered.

"Yes and no, now that you ask," Hobbs replied.

Ferguson and Kelly exchanged puzzled glances, then looked at the young squire. "'Yes and no'?" asked the Scot. "What do you mean?"

"Today began on a rather odd note for me," said Hobbs. "First thing this fine morning, a troubled young lady came to my office."

Again, Kelly and Ferguson looked at each. "Well, Hobbs?" the former asked. "What did she want?"

"Deuced if I can fathom it. My visitor was a young maid from New Zealand. She had just been to Cornwall to call on an old friend who lives in some obscure little hamlet. What was the name? Ah, yes—in Maidenwell."

His listeners said nothing, as Hobbs retold Janet Miller's story. When he ended, they looked at him, then at each other.

Their manner was noticeably non-committal, their faces unmoving. Then, Kelly, ever the misogynist, spoke. "She's obviously hysterical and distraught," he said. "She would do best to follow her friend's advice and return home."

"That was my own view," Hobbs confessed. "I told her as much. But, can we really dismiss her so easily as an hyster-ical woman? What if there proves to be some truth to her tale?"

Quietly and calmly, Sean Ferguson walked back to his desk. He stood there, silent and pensive, his hands clasped, with his thumbs hooked into his belt. "She said that she would be back here Monday morning? She must be expecting some sort of miracle from you, Hobbs."

"So it seems. But what am I to do?"

"Obviously," replied Ferguson. "Find evidence to support her fears. Prove that something dark and diabolical has happened in Maidenwell— that her friend has fallen prey to foul, sinister forces. Even if there is no evidence, you are to find it; even if her fears are groundless, you are to give them foundation."

As the two men talked, Kelly knitted his brow. "Hmm," he muttered, shaking his head. "Hmm—yes. Curious coinci-dence."

"Is something wrong?" asked the Scot.

"I'm not sure. I was just thinking of an odd coincidence. The first victim in our own case—Sgt. Bailey told us that she lived in Maidenwell."

"Yes, so he did," Ferguson recalled.

Poor Hobbs felt left out in the cold during their brief exchange. "Would you chaps mind filling me in?" he asked.

"No, not at all," Ferguson quietly answered. "Are you aware of the case that Kelly and I are working on? Well, the first victim was a young woman from Maidenwell."

"Maidenwell? Are you sure?"

"Positive," Kelly assured him, as he tapped the folder containing the data on the case.

"That is odd—very odd," noted Hobbs. "But it might be merely coincidental."

Slowly, he got up, and turned to leave. He paused momentarily, as he reached for the doorknob.

"Yes," he said, thinking aloud. "I think that a call to Sgt. Bailey is in order. First thing tomorrow morning."

"A good man," Kelly told him. "We've worked with him before. You will let us know what you learn, won't you?"

"Why, upon my honor, of course I shall," Hobbs readily assured him. "Professional courtesy, old boy."

He smiled a warm, broad smile, then opened the door and left.

CHAPTER 21

▼

A TASK OF HIS OWN

There was a clear, star-filled sky overhead, as another cold, crisp winter's night descended upon Cornwall. Eliezer Jordan had not seen or done as much as he had wanted to that afternoon. His first impulse, when he returned to his room at the guesthouse, was to reproach himself for not having done more.

Removing his shoes from his tired feet, he paused for a moment, and realized that he really had no cause to be harsh with himself. After all, he had arrived in England only yesterday. This was his first afternoon in Cornwall and on the case. Even he, who had witnessed a few miracles in his lifetime, could not expect to solve any case after only one cold, rather shocking, afternoon.

He smiled, and shook his head. Then the smile faded, and a serious, almost vengeful look came to his face. Now he had seen the killer's cruel handiwork at first-hand. He had come to the scene of the crime soon after the crime had been com-mitted.

This was now not longer an 'interesting case'—it had become personal. And it was no longer just a police matter—Jordan now saw it as his mission—a task of his own—to put an end to a dangerous predator's loathsome activities.

How close had he and his opponent come to meeting? An hour? Two? Surely not more than three, from what Rev. Thompson had said about his own movements.

"There's little else that I can do, tonight," he thought. "But I have a few long, busy days ahead of me—no doubt of that."

Now, as he felt the fatigue and jet lag setting in, he went downstairs, to make a quick phone-call. He dialed a number in London; a voice with a slight Scottish burr answered.

"Sean? Jordan here," said the caller, in a low tone. "I'm in Liskeard. No, I don't know when I'll be back. Listen—there's been another one. You'd better call a Sgt. Bailey, of the Bodmin Police. Late this morning, or early this afternoon. Found in the church—in the vicar's study. Must have been only a few hours before I got there. Yes, I'll be careful," he promised.

Returning the phone to its cradle, he went back to his room, where he fell quickly and easily asleep. As he slept, three of the people he sought were talking in the sitting room of an old, well-kept cottage at the other end of Cornwall.

CHAPTER 22

▼

IN REDRUTH

"Don't forget the meeting in Redruth on Sunday," Malcolm
Morgan was saying.

"Redruth? Oh, yes. Thanks for reminding me. I had almost forgotten,"
Barrett replied, as he put on his heavy down jacket. "Do you really think
anything will come of it?"

"That's hard to say. After all, there hasn't been an archdruid, or a council of druids, in Britain for sixteen centuries. And from what I've seen and
heard, the various circles simply don't think or act in terms of unity and
cooperation.

"Then, why try it?"

"Perhaps because it's never been done. And I believe that we must do
whatever we can, to reclaim and preserve our past."

"Well, it will be interesting to see how the others react to your suggestions. I'll be here in the morning." With those words, Barrett walked out
into the cold night air, and made his way home.

A few days later, members of several druidic circles arrived in Redruth, to meet at the home of Alice Penrose, the well-known sculptress. They had all come to the old religion in different ways. Some, like Llewellyn Cardigan, had a quiet, sincere pride in their ancient heritage. For others, like Malcolm Morgan and Andrew Barrett, it was as much a matter of stubborn rebelliousness as anything else.

Still others, like Alice Penrose, took a dilettante's approach to life; for them, it was rather chic to don flowing robes, and copper pendants etched with mystical symbols, and gather in solemn assembly at many of Britain's circles.

After her guests had arrived and spent some time in idle chatter, Miss Penrose clapped her hands to get their atten-tion.

"I've invited you all here at the behest of Malcolm Morgan, whom some of you know. He has already told me of his marvelous idea; I've called you here that he might share it with you. Malcolm," she said, as she turned her beaming face to the druid.

Now the center of attention, Morgan came directly to the point.

"Friends, my suggestion is a simple one. There are some two hundred Druidic circles throughout Britain. Until now, we have each gone our sep-arate ways. There has never been any co-operation or co-ordination between us.

"I would like to remedy this by reviving the office of archdruid, and have him aided by a council of druids. I would like us to pool our energies and resources, in pre-serving the ancient ways, and marking the four great fes-tivals together."

Morgan paused. With an air of self-assuredness, he gazed at his audi-ence and let them absorb his remarks.

A flurry of questions arose.

"A Druidic council? Who would serve on it? What would its duties be? And its powers? How would the archdruid be chosen? What of his powers and duties? How would our autonomy be affected?"

These questions, and others, came from the people in Alice Penrose's sitting room. But among those gathered there that day, one man was very silent, and very skeptical.

Llewellyn Cardigan frowned. His mind examined Morgan's proposal. "So, he wants to set up a druidic council, does he? For what purpose, I wonder?" Cardigan's face twisted cynically. "Does he see himself as archdruid?" he wondered, as one particular face now caught his attention.

Llewellyn Cardigan and Andrew Barrett noticed each other almost simultaneously, and both now felt their anger aroused, but neither acted upon that anger.

Now Cardigan no longer felt himself a detached observer.

"Would you mind answering some questions, Mr. Morgan?" he ventured to ask, speaking for the first time that day.

"Certainly not," the druid replied. "What is it?"

"It's a matter of who will serve as archdruid. Assuming, of course, that this plan of yours becomes a reality. Whom did you have in mind? Yourself, perhaps?"

"I would serve if the council chose me."

Cardigan rubbed his chin. "I see. Well, as you say, there are many druidic circles in Britain. Some may choose to join you; others may not. How would you feel about those who might vote to stay separate, or set up their own council?"

Before Morgan replied, Barrett stepped over and whispered something in his ear. That action answered many questions for Cardigan. He almost ignored Morgan's response.

"If a druid other than myself were chosen, I would honour that choice, and follow him. Just as I expect the council's choice to be honored if I were elected."

He looked at Cardigan with an unflinching expression.

"Now, as to your other question—I don't intend to create any discord among the followers of the Old Religion. Quite the contrary—my aim is to foster harmony and unity amongst us. But if any should decide not to join us—whether or not they set up a rival council—it will be they, and not I, who imperil our noble cause. And as all here know, we have been disunited and powerless for far too long."

Feeling his temper slowly rising, Morgan paused, in an effort to maintain his composure.

Cardigan sensed his discomfort, and said no more. Decid-ing that he had seen and heard enough, he took his leave of his hostess. He returned to St. Ives, not knowing if, when, or where he would cross verbal swords with Morgan and Barrett again.

CHAPTER 23

▼

THE ANTLERED GOD

It was a blustery Saturday morning. Winter's icy fingers continued to give all of Britain a bone-chilling massage. Despite the harsh weather, people throughout the realm roused themselves from slumber, and with their characteristic stubbornness, they braved the elements to go about their daily affairs.

In a comfortable room in a Liskeard guest-house, Eliezer Jordan was emerging from a deep, refreshing sleep. It was 8:15, on his second morning in England. He slowly opened his eyes, sat up, and rubbed his face.

As full consciousness returned, he recalled where he was, and why he had come there. He got out of bed, washed, and dressed. He had breakfast, then put on his heavy down coat, and the beige woolen cap and scarf that his eldest daughter had knitted for him.

Walking briskly to the car that he had hired, he turned on the ignition, and drove the icy roads back to Bodmin. Forty minutes later, he parked the car a short distance from the church. For the second time in two days, he approached the edifice, eager to pursue his investigation.

He entered, walked to the vicar's study, and knocked on the door. A voice from within bade him enter. He opened the door, and quietly walked in. The vicar sat at his desk. He wore a look of anxiety on his face. A small brandy was in his hand, in an effort to steady his nerves.

"Mr. Thomson? What's wrong?" the visitor asked. The vicar, obviously upset, knitted his brow, and looked at the newcomer. "Yes? Oh, yes—the American with Scotland Yard. Please come in—sit down."

The vicar waved his hand towards a chair. Removing his coat, Jordan accepted the invitation. Seated, he let his eyes wander around the room. Books on a variety of subjects filled some shelves. A few potted plants were hanging on one of the walls. Some books on gardening and herbalism rested on a windowsill.

Jordan studied his host for the first time. Matthew Thomson had spent the past fifteen of his forty-seven years as a clergyman. He was no stranger to hard work, having been a farm hand, a veterinarian, and a gunner's mate in the Royal Navy, before coming home to Bodmin and his present calling.

He impressed Jordan as a peaceful, good-natured man—a man of inner strength on whom his parishioners could depend. His discovery of the mutilated body had tested that strength, and strained Thomson's peaceful nature. Even Jordan had not yet fully recovered from that sight.

The vicar filled two cups with brandy. He gave one to Jordan, then sat down.

"Why are you interested in these murders?" he asked. "And why are you looking for the murderer?"

Jordan smiled faintly. "I'm an archaeologist by profes-sion," he began. "Two friends of mine are with Scotland Yard. Last week one of them phoned me, and asked me I could help in some way."

"Curious," Thomson observed, as he leaned back in his chair. Then, after a brief silence, he reached for an envelope on his desk, and handed it to Jordan.

"Perhaps I shouldn't give this to you—I mean, the police will have to see it. I found this when I came to church this morning. It had been slipped through the mail-slot on the side door."

Thomson came to a decision and extended the envelope.

Jordan took it, opened it, and removed its contents. He was holding three sheets of drawing paper. On each was a finely executed pen-and-ink sketch.

He admired the keen eye and steady hand of the artist, but that was all. He didn't know what to make of them—the images meant nothing to him. He admitted as much as he gave them back to the vicar.

"What do they mean?" he asked.

"What do you know about Cornwall?" Thomson asked him.

"Very little, I'm afraid—aside from its severe winters, and the legend surrounding Tintagel as King Arthur's seat," Jordan replied. "I had heard something about its clay and tin mines—which the Greeks and Etruscans supposedly knew of, 2500 years ago."

The vicar got up and refilled their cups. "Cornwall has always been last in England," he began. "The last part to be Romanized, Anglicized, and Christianized. And the Reforma-tion and Industrial Revolution spread through the rest of England, before coming here."

He paused briefly, looked pensively at the drawings, then said, "The ways of our Celtic ancestors—language, lore, and religion—have survived longer in Cornwall than anywhere in Europe. Many of my neighbors still speak the old language; others know many of the tales of the ancient gods and heroes."

A cloud came over his features. "Whoever drew these sketches knows those stories," he said, grimly.

He pointed to one. "This is the dreaded Balor—'Balor of the Baleful Eye.'"

"A strange epithet," Jordan observed.

"Balor was a king of the Fomorians, a terrifying race of aboriginal giants living in Ireland," Thompson explained. "As a young child, he sneaked a look at his father's druids while they were brewing charms. The strong fumes of the brew entered his eye and poisoned it. From that day onward, nothing could ever survive the eye's fearful glance. In Celtic lore, Balor was the very embodiment of the evil eye. Wherever he went, four men followed him, to lift his eyelid by passing a handle through the edge."

"A delightful fellow, wasn't he? What became of him?"

"He was finally killed. He was a leader of the giants at the Battle of Mag Tured. His grandson, Lugh, led his oppo-nents, the Tuatha de Danaan, the 'People of the Goddess Dana,' who mastered the arts of druidry and magic. Just as Balor's eyelid was being raised, Lugh hurled a stone from his sling; it killed Balor, carried the eye out though the back of his head, and killed twenty-seven of Balor's men."

Jordan recalled another giant killed by a sling, but that was a different land and people. Then, he asked, "What of the other sketches? This one looks like a collage, with women of various ages."

"Have you ever heard of the banshee?"

"Only the word. I don't know what it refers to."

"The SIDE are the fairy-folk of Irish folklore. The bean side—'Woman of the Side'—could be either a beautiful maiden, weeping over a coming death, or an old hag, fore-telling it. The banshee was often spoken of as the 'washer of the ford.' Legend had it that a person about to die saw her at a ford, washing a bloody garment."

Silent and immobile, Jordan sat there, and studied the three foreboding sketches. "What about this last one?" he finally asked. "What does it mean?"

"The horned figure in the middle is Cernunnos, the Horned One. I remember seeing pictures of him in books of Celtic lore, when I was a boy. He was a Celtic deity, always por-trayed with antlers, and seated cross-legged, as he is here, with a great stag to his right, and holding a ram-headed serpent in his left hand."

He paused briefly.

"Cernunnos was the horned dweller of the subterranean Celtic nether-world," he continued. "He was a very popular deity. I've heard that two towns in Brittany—Cornouialle, and Carnac—recall this god, and his name. In fact, the people of Carnac still hold an annual festival in honor of St. Cornely, patron saint of horned animals."

"And here in Britain?" Jordan asked. "Are there any customs or celebrations that might stem from his worship?"

Thomson knitted his brow, and shook his head. "No, I'm sorry. I can't think of any."

Then, his face lit up. "Yes, there might be one. It's called the 'Festival of the Deer-men.' It's held each year in Abbotts Bromley, in Staffordshire, every 4 September."

Now it was Jordan's turn to be surprised. "September 4? Are you sure of the date?"

"Yes. Why?"

"Just thinking of an odd coincidence," Jordan replied, as he reached into the pocket of his shirt, and removed a slip of paper. "Yes, a very odd coincidence," he muttered, as he confirmed his memory.

The American now looked at his watch and noticed that the morning was almost gone. "Well, Mr. Thomson, I hadn't meant to take up to much of your time," he apologized."

"Quite the contrary—your visit was most timely. I need-ed something to help calm me down, after this ghastly experi-ence."

Jordan put on his coat, and opened the door. "You've been very helpful, Mr. Thomson. Perhaps, some day, I can return the favor."

"If you can help stop the killings—bring the killer to justice—that will repay me many times over," the vicar assured him.

Thomson walked down the hallway with Jordan. At the door, he uttered a word of caution to the American.

"Take care, my friend," he said. "You are up against a deadly opponent."
"Thanks for the warning—and the hot chocolate. I'll be
careful," Jordan promised.

"What a way to spend a Saturday morning," Jordan thought, as he
headed for his car. He glanced back over his shoulder at the church. "Balor
of the Dreadful Eye—banshees—antlered gods—ram-headed serpents,"
he thought. "What next?"

CHAPTER 24

▼

GRUESOME NEWS

Sean Ferguson returned the earpiece of the phone to the cradle. His hand still held it firmly as his mouth tensed angrily. He stood there, thought quickly and deeply for half-a-minute, then picked up the receiver again, and dialed a number.

"Yes? John Kelly here," a voice at the other end answered.

"Good. Can you spare a few moments?"

"Yes—of course," said Kelly, as he put aside the man-dolin that he had been playing. "What is it?"

"Jordan just rang. From Liskeard. There's been another one," said Ferguson, grimly.

Kelly was shocked and speechless.

"Good God!" he exclaimed, when he found his voice. "Did he give you any details?"

"Very few, I'm afraid. The body was found in the Bodmin church. In the vicar's study. Jordan figured that he and the murderer missed each other by only a couple of hours."

"In Bodmin, eh? That means our old friend, Sgt. Bailey," Kelly observed. "We'd better ring him first thing in the morning. Would you mind if I tell Hobbs about this?" he asked, almost as an afterthought.

"Hobbs? Why?"

"I'm thinking of that story that he told us, and of an interesting coincidence."

Ferguson wrinkled his brow. "Hmm. I really hadn't thought of it. I suppose it won't do any harm. After all, Hobbs was planning to ring Bailey, to check on it. You might be right. Ask him to join us in our office first thing tomorrow morning," he said, then hung up.

At that moment, the front door opened—it was Peggy Fer-guson returning from her shift at the hospital. Without a word, she hung up her coat, went to the kitchen, and prepared a cup of tea.

Sean Ferguson wore a grim look on his face as he walked slowly towards the kitchen. He stood in the doorway, wrapped in worried thought.

After twenty-two years of marriage, Peggy was very much aware of her husband's many moods, as he was of hers. Quietly, she walked over and kissed him gently on the cheek.

"You're up late, dear. Care for some tea?"

"Tea? No—no, thank you. It may keep me awake. And you should keep away from it at this hour—especially after a long day at the hospital. How was it today?"

"Three children brought in with measles, and two adults with TB." She ran her fingers through her hair, and took another sip of tea. Lovingly, she put a hand on her husband's face.

"You look so worn out, dear. What is it? It's that same awful case, isn't it, Sean?"

Involuntarily, the man shuddered, and clenched his fists.

"Jordan just rang," he said, in a hushed tone. "He was in Bodmin this afternoon. There's been another one."

Her cup fell from her hand, as she began to tremble.

"Dear God! When will it stop? What did he say? Is he safe?"

"Yes, he's safe," he assured her. Instinctively, they held each other. It was at times like these that they appreciated the comfort and support that they could give each other—something that was so basic to their relationship.

He poured a glass of juice, and drank it slowly.

"I just rang Kelly," he told her. "We'll meet at the Yard in the morning—ring Sgt. Bailey, and take it from there."

"What will you do, Sean?" she asked him. Then, she laughed nervously, and said, "If I know you, the two of you will follow Eli, and go to Cornwall yourselves."

Her husband smiled wanly, and laughed a short, nervous laugh.

"We may have to do just that," he replied, with a heavy sigh. Gently, she put her arms around his neck, and kissed him. "I don't know about you, but I've had a long, hard day. I'm going to bed. So should you, dear."

"Hmm? Yes—of course," he mumbled. He stood there, moodily, for a few minutes, before following her to bed.

"Damn!" he grumbled. "There must be some pattern to this hellish business! What can it be?! And when will this bloody flesher slip up?!"

"Another one," he thought, as he went upstairs, to bed.

"Damned bloody bastard."

CHAPTER 25

▼

WITH FERGUSON AND KELLY

Sean Ferguson awoke early the next morning. He dressed quietly and quickly, so as not to disturb his wife. The mood of self-pity that he had begun to feel last night had left him, but his nagging frustration and grim determination had not.

Leaving the house on Kenneth Crescent, he walked to the nearby tube station. It was still early when he arrived at the Yard and went up to his office.

Removing his coat, he sat down, and dialed Bodmin's police station. The phone rang six times before someone answered it.

"Bodmin Police—Constable Franklin speaking."

"This is Ferguson of the Yard. Is Sgt. Bailey in yet?"

"Sorry, sir. He hasn't come in yet. Can I help you?"

"Perhaps. I heard that there was another murder yesterday. I'd like to know the details."

After a moment's hesitation Franklin said, "I suppose you'll get a report anyway. Our local vicar rang here just before three in the afternoon—said it was urgent. Sgt. Bailey is one of his parishioners; he hurried over, and found a dead man in the pastor's study. Hands and feet had been cut off; they were then placed on a wreath in a wicker basket. That's the long and the short of it, Sir."

"Who was the dead man?"

"Albert Stedman. Nice enough bloke. He was a gardener and lived in Helland. He was a member of Mr. Thomson's flock until about six years ago."

"Hmm. Thank you, Constable," said Ferguson, just as the door of his office opened.

John Kelly entered, followed by Mr. Hobbs.

"Will that be all, sir?" asked Franklin.

"For the moment. Please have Sgt. Bailey ring me directly he comes in. Tell him that it's about Maidenwell. Thanks."

He put down the phone, and looked at his two anxious colleagues. He wore a look of eager anticipation on his normally subdued features.

"Kelly told me the ghastly news," said Hobbs. "Well, old boy? What do we do, now?"

"I'm not going to sit here, waiting helplessly for him to strike again," said the Scot, as he filled and lit his first pipe of the day. "I'll wait until I hear from Bailey, and see if another friend calls with any information. Then we'll be in a better position to act."

"A trip to Bodmin might be in order," Hobbs suggested.

"Possibly," said Kelly, as he poured some herbal tea for himself and his two colleagues. "But that would mean going over old ground. After all, we've already been out there. Bailey has been doing his best. And Jordan is out there now."

"True enough," Ferguson agreed, as he sipped the warm, healthful liquid. "Sometimes it might be both helpful and necessary to retrace one's steps. There may be some new data, or a fresh perspective."

"Or another blasted killing," Hobbs added, gloomily. Then, a puzzled look came to his face. "I say—have you discovered anything important?"

"Only the story that you told us yesterday, and the one that Constable Franklin just told me," he said, as he repeated the account of the latest atrocity.

A weighty silence filled the room, after Ferguson finished his story. As they sat there, he removed a sheet of blank paper from a drawer of his desk. Shifting his position slightly, he wriggled his fingers, then began to fold the paper.

An understanding smile came to Kelly's face, and a look of bewilderment to Hobbs', as Sean Ferguson continued his folding. Three minutes later, he gently placed the finished product in the center of his desk and studied it with an air of quiet pride.

"There," he said, with a smile of satisfaction. "Not bad—not bad at all."

"Very well. But what is it? And why do it?" asked Hobbs.

"It's a Masinois," Ferguson replied. "One of three varieties of Belgian hunting dog. As to 'why'—well, call it a form of therapy. A way to keep my equilibrium—an aid to concentration."

Hobbs shook his head, as his two friends smiled contentedly. "You know, you really ought to have some creative interests," Kelly suggested. "After all, Ferguson has his origami—I have my mandolin and harpsichord. Sherlock Holmes kept bees," he noted, as he poured another cup of tea.

Hobbs smiled a self-conscious smile. "I do have something of a hobby, now that you mention it," he replied.

"No! Really?"

"Really. In fact, I have two. This may come as a surprise to you, but I've become rather adept at needlepoint. I've done all the patterns that you've seen hanging on the walls of my flat. And I've been studying skrimshaw for—let me see—yes, for three-and-a-half years, now." he said, beaming with pride.

"Well, bless dear Mother MacFarland," Kelly gasped, in genuine surprise. "I should never have guessed it."

"Nor I," the Scot echoed.

Further discussion was cut off by the ringing of the phone. Kelly answered it.

"Yes? Kelly here. Ah—Sgt. Bailey—how nice to hear from you."

"I'm sure it is," the Cornishman replied. He had had little sleep these past three days, and his mood at the moment, was not very light. "My constable tells me that you rang earlier—mentioned something about Maidenwell and the body found in our local church. How did you learn about it so quickly? And what do you want to know about Maidenwell?"

"A friend of ours was in Bodmin. He arrived at the church just as you were leaving. When he saw what had happened, he rang Ferguson with the news."

"Really? Well, in that case, Inspector, how can we be of help to each other?"

"There's something I'm curious to know," said Ferguson, who had picked up his own phone. "Were there any peculiar marks on the body? Aside from the fatal wounds, that is."

Lodging his phone between his head and shoulder, Bailey began to toy with the hand-crafted brigantine that he kept on his desk.

"Queer markings? Let me see."

He thought of the post-mortem that he had witnessed, a short while ago. Then, "Yes, there was something odd, now that you ask," he said. "There was a tattoo on the back of the neck. Near the trapezius. It was about three-quarters-of-an-inch long. The doctor didn't notice it until she was nearly done."

"What sort of tattoo?" asked Kelly.

"I don't know quite what to make of it. It looked like something a child might draw."

"Anything specific?"

"Yes, come to think of it. I'd hazard a guess and call it a spotted serpent with elk's horns."

CHAPTER 26

▼

FOLLOWING A THREAD

Quiet and unobtrusive, Eliezer Jordan sat at a table in a corner of one of Bodmin's pubs. As he ate a fresh salad, he found it difficult not to think of the case. Sipping his coffee, he saw in his mind's eye the sketches that Rev. Thomson had received.

"Well, at least it hasn't been dull," he thought to himself. "My dream, yesterday morning—a dead body, mutilated just as I had dreamed—now, these strange sketches. There has to be some common denominator—but what is it? Where and how do I find it?"

He sat in silence, the fingers of his left hand tapping out a melody on the table. "Thirteen killings," he thought, as he began to arrange those pieces of the puzzle that he now had. "The first was on September 5—the body was found in the Bodmin churchyard. A day after—what was it? Yes—the 'Festival of the Deermen', in Abbott's Bromley. A coincidence? Maybe, but it might be worth checking."

Placing his elbows on the table, he held his face in his hands and continued the process. "Two bodies found in Bodmin; two in the middle of

London; two in Northumberland; one in Somerset; three in Wiltshire; two in Warwickshire; and one in Gloucestershire. Whoever the killer is, he certainly moves around a lot. Assuming, of course, that there is only one."

He grimaced, and shook his head in disgust. "There has to be a pattern–there **has** to be!" he silently muttered.

Moments later, he got up, paid his bill, and went outside. As was his practice when working on a puzzle, he began to talk to himself. "I'm looking for a needle in a haystack. Well, at least I have a piece of thread. May as well follow it, and see if it leads anywhere."

A visit to the local library turned up some interesting items on Cornwall's history, geography, and folklore. A cursory glance through some books on the ancient Celts merely repeated what he had learned from the vicar.

"Can I help you, sir?" asked a librarian, when she saw the look of annoyance on the visitor's face.

"Possibly. I'm looking for information on two mythological figures—Balor, and Cernunnos. I've found something, but not enough, I'm afraid."

Accustomed to dealing with a variety of curious questions, the librarian soon found some material for him. "Here you are. I hope they can help you."

"Thanks much. So do I," he said, with a warm smile. It never hurt to be kind to librarians when doing research—or to people in general.

As he took the books, he noticed a peculiar expression in the librarian's eyes.

"Is something wrong, Miss?" he asked her.

"Oh—excuse me, sir. I didn't mean to stare. It's just that there's something hauntingly familiar about you—I'm certain that I've seen your face before. Very recently, in fact."

"Really? That's odd—I've never been here before," the man assured her.

Almost automatically, she went to her desk, and removed something from her handbag. It was a copy of a book called HOUNDS AND JACKALS—A

HISTORY OF GAMES IN THE ANCIENT NEAR EAST. On the back cover was a photograph of the author—Eliezer Jordan.

With a self-conscious smile, she showed it to him. "Would it be a bother to ask for your autograph? It's for my 10-year-old niece. She's already ready your books on underwater archaeology, and on the archaeology of the southern Sudan—she even says that you got her to want to be an archaeologist."

"Really? I'd be delighted to sign it for her," said Jordan. "What's her name?"

"Lisa. Lisa Mainwaring."

Jordan took out a pen, inscribed the book for the young girl, then went to a table, and sat down. He checked the indexes of the books the librarian had given him, then read the assorted references.

It was not long before he sat up, and his face brightened. "Ah, yes! Very interesting," he thought, as he made some quick notes.

"Unexpectedly helpful," he told the librarian, when he returned the books. "I appreciate your help. And I hope that Lisa enjoys the book."

He smiled a warm smile, then turned and left.

Chapter 27

▼

You Look Worried

As Jordan drove back to Liskeard, a husband and wife were hard at work on their farm in Maidenwell. With their usual silence and efficiency, they went about their daily chores.

All morning, and into the early afternoon, they did their work without exchanging a word, or a single glance. At last, they ended their labors, and walked slowly back to the cottage that had been the Woodson home for several generations. Only after entering its confines did they finally speak.

"Will you go to the meeting in Redruth tomorrow, Jim?" Gwen asked her husband.

"Redruth? Oh, yes—Malcolm's meeting. Yes, I'll go. I'm curious to see what comes of it."

"So am I," said his wife, as they went upstairs, removed their work-clothes, and washed. Gwen tied her hair in a bun to scrub her face, as she said, "Though I'm not as optimistic as Malcolm. There are too many Druidic circles in Britain—we have no political or economic power. And there are too many 'me too's' dabbling in the Old Religion, to my way of thinking."

"Like Alice Penrose?" her husband asked, with a sly smile.

"Especially Alice Penrose. She may dangle a few meaningless pendants around her neck and hold some silly 'soiree', acting out parts of the Mabinogion, and have a replica of the Mast of Maccha over her fireplace, but that's all."

"Aye." Jim agreed. "She's as devoted to the old religion as we are to the new. And that ridiculous portrait of her, posing as Medhbh, leading her warriors in pursuit of the great bull—hmph!" he snorted.

"The ceremony went rather well," said Gwen, after they had sat down to tea. "Though I don't see why Albert was chosen as the sacrifice. He was your friend—you introduced him to paganism. Did Malcolm tell you anything?"

"He said something about Ellen having had another dream—a dream in which she saw Albert's name, written in the alphabet of Ogma."

"So—it was Ellen, again," Gwen cynically noted. "I don't like her, Jim. I never have. She may have the gift, but she seems to have too much influence over Malcolm."

"You'd think her knitting needles were divining rods," said her husband. "Even during our ceremonies, she weaves patterns in the air with them, like some spirit let lose at Samhuin."

He grimaced slightly, and laughed a short laugh. "But she is dedicated to the cause—I'll say that much for her."

Now, he got up from the table, walked over to the fireplace, and lit a fire. He watched as the flames grew, and listened to their crisp cackling. His wife joined him, and they both lit cigarettes.

"You look worried, Jim," she observed. "What is it?"

The man didn't answer right away. Instead, he began to thumb through a copy of the 'Book of Invasions', an old and cherished part of the ancient Celtic heritage. He thumbed through it, but gave neither the text, nor the rich illustrations, much thought. He tossed his cigarette into the fire, then lit another.

"I was thinking about the constable who stopped by here, two days ago," he finally said. "And that girl from New Zealand, who came asking for you."

"It's only a mild nuisance. Nothing more. No need to fret about it," Gwen said, as she poured a cup of warm tea for each of them.

"She was rather cheeky, if you ask me," Woodson went on. "After all, how long has it been since you stopped writing to her?"

"Two years, I think. Perhaps three," was her reply, after a very brief moment of recollection.

"And you didn't invite her to our wedding," he reminded her. Pausing, her added a small bit of liquor to his tea, for extra flavor and punch. He sipped it carefully, to test the mixture. "Hmm—just right. You really ought to try it," he suggested.

"No, thank you. I tried it once—I don't really fancy that concoction of yours."

There was a brief, awkward silence. Then the woman picked up some needlepoint that she had begun, and worked on it with skill and patience.

"You really can't blame me," she finally said. "After all, I purposely didn't meet her at the railway station. And when she found her way here, didn't I insist that she leave?"

"Yes, you did. Cheeky wench," her husband muttered. "Going to the police—I'll wager that's why he came here."

"No doubt," Gwen agreed, without interrupting her work. "But what is there to lead anyone to believe that these deaths are all actually ritual sacrifices? Or suspect that we're in any way responsible for them? We've been very careful, dear," she reassured him. "We left no clues. The police will never be able to find any pattern to the deaths. Or any motive for them."

She put a comforting hand on his arm, and smiled a confidant, contented smile. "Really, Jim—you're worrying needlessly. No one will ever identify us. Or discover why we've done what we've done."

James Woodson looked at his wife, and silently wondered. After all, she, too, has the gift of sacred vision, he reminded himself. He had learned to trust her insights as well as his own sound instincts.

Sitting down in an armchair, he placed his drink on the floor next to him. Once again, he opened his copy of Leabhar Gabhala Eireann, 'The Book of the Invasions of Ireland.'

He read on, enjoying both his drink, and the epic that told of the coming of the Gaels to Ireland.

And in the back of his mind, he wondered why Sgt. Bailey had bothered coming to Maidenwell, and why the policeman had knocked on the door of his cottage.

CHAPTER 28

▼

JOHN KELLY'S MUSINGS

Despite his fatigue, Sgt. Bailey listened to Hobbs's story. "Obstinate, isn't she?" was his only comment, at the end of the Inspector's tale.

"True enough," Hobbs agreed. "And very insistent."

Sgt. Bailey cradled the phone on his left shoulder, carefully brushed his mustache, then returned to the matter at hand.

"The poor girl is obviously distraught," he said, sharing with them the conclusion that he had reached three days earlier. "I went to the house in Maidenwell and found nothing to arouse any suspicions.

"I don't doubt your judgment," said Hobbs, after Bailey recounted the events of that wet, windy morning. "The young lady will be returning here Monday morning. I simply wanted to confer with you—to benefit from your own experience, as it were."

"Naturally, Inspector. It's a fairly routine matter, as I see it. She's making a mountain out of a molehill, if you ask me." "Very well, then. You've been most helpful, sir. Very kind of you. Thank you," said Hobbs, as the conversation came to an end.

Kelly was leaning against the edge of his desk, his arms folded across his chest. He wore a bemused look on his face, as he listened to the brief exchange between Bailey and Hobbs.

"Well, gentlemen? What have we learned today?" Ferguson asked his two colleagues. "Have we made any progress this fine Arctic morn?"

He puffed leisurely on his pipe, but his outward appearance contrasted with the anger and anxiety that he had been feeling, these past three months.

"Ferguson, what do you know about tattoos?" asked Kelly, after a brief silence.

"Tattoos? Very little, I'm afraid. Only that the practice is said to go back many thousands of years. It's supposed to be almost as old as the human race—which should extend its lineage back several millennia or so, I should say. Why?"

"Curiosity, of course," was the simple reply. "Did you know that there are three-hundred-seventeen tattooing emporia in Greater London?" he asked his friends.

"No! Really?" asked a genuinely surprised Clovis Hobbs.

"Three hundred?"

"And seventeen. Yes, Hobbs."

"Where did you learn this vital statistic?" asked Fergu-son, as he cleaned the bowl of his pipe. "From your dear Mother MacFarland?"

"Yes, if you must know," replied Kelly, a bit peeved by his friend's tone.

"Very well—I'll take your word for it," said the Scot, as he stood by the window. "But why mention it?"

"Because Bailey told you that the latest victim had a tattoo of a spotted serpent."

"Tattoos?" asked Hobbs. "Spotted serpents? Is that significant?"

"It's possible, Hobbs. What does the image conjure up in your mind?"

"The Sherlock Holmes, tale, 'The Speckled Band,'" said Hobbs. "It was a swamp adder, if I'm not mistaken—the deadliest snake in India."

"There's also the serpent in Eden," Ferguson added. "The embodiment of evil, in Christianity."

"Very curious," Hobbs observed. "A couple of chaps I knew at University were into metaphysics—Madame Blavatsky and all that. I heard them speak of the serpent as the symbol of great cosmic wisdom."

"Well, gentlemen," said Ferguson, "since you're more interested in ancient symbols than in modern forensics, let's not forget the caduceus."

Now, it was the turn of Kelly and Hobbs to register looks of surprise. "The caduceus?" asked the latter.

"Yes, Hobbs. Two snakes entwined around an upright staff. It's the accepted symbol of the medical profession. But where does any of this leave us? What could it possibly have to do with our problem?"

CHAPTER 29

▼

A STRANGE VISION

It was late afternoon by the time Jordan got back to Liskeard. He went up to his room at the guesthouse, and hung up his coat. Sitting on the edge of the bed, he removed his shoes and rubbed his feet. Slowly, pensively, he ran his fingers through his bushy brown hair.

"Well, the day certainly hasn't been dull. Or wasted," he reflected, after he washed and dried his hands and face. "I think I'll skip dinner tonight. I have something more important to do, right now; eating will just be a hindrance."

He sat down, and chose to follow the sage advice that his grandmother had given him, many years before. "First, you eat. Then, you sit back, rest, and digest your food."

He smiled as he recalled her words.

"And it's as true of mental food as it is of physical food," he had long since learned. "But I don't think that she had murder cases—or the Kabbalah—in mind when she told me that."

With that, he reached into his well-worn nylon tote bag. One by one, he carefully withdrew his 'tools of the trade,' and placed them on the bed.

That done, he plugged the power-cord of the cassette player into an outlet, and put a cassette into the machine. On the back of his head he placed the brown woolen skullcap that his eldest daughter had knitted for him. Then he covered his shoulders with the beige woolen prayer shawl that his wife had made. On it she had embroidered a diagram of the ten Divine Attributes, as taught by the mystical tradition.

He removed his shoes, and turned on the cassette player. Closing his eyes, he started to breathe slowly and deeply, and began to pray. A strange transformation soon took place, in that cozy little room. The first faint intoxicating strains of music had barely begun to caress his mind when Eliezer Jordan, archaeologist and scholar, glided effortlessly aside, to be replaced by another, more mysterious being.

From deep within, a mystical force emerged, moving to the fore like some swirling wraith. It was Eliezer Jordan who had entered that room and closed his eyes in prayer. Now, it was Barad, the master of the unknown, who opened his eyes, and went in search of answers.

The figure continued his praying. As melody followed melody, the mystic focused his thoughts upon an ancient symbol—the Tree of the Knowledge of Good and Evil. The image was faint and distant, at first, barely perceptible even to his sensitive inner eye.

"No need to rush," he told himself. "If a vision is to come, it will come at the proper time. And it will be a specific one, for a specific purpose."

With a patience born of experience, he waited, and prayed.

The music played on, as his mystical state deepened.

Now, he saw a pale silver sphere fall from the branch of a tree. It hung suspended in mid-air for several seconds, the floated towards him. It approached, the paused, and hovered just beyond his reach.

It shimmered with a soft, pulsating light, emitting thin rays of red, blue, green, and silver light. The shimmering soon ceased and Barad could see his image reflected on its polished surface.

"A raging storm," he suddenly sensed. "Yes—it's a storm at sea. And an ancient sailing ship battered and tossed by the fury of the waves.

The strange vision continued and Barad watched, as something was tossed overboard. It was a man who was tossed into the raging waters, soon to be swallowed by some huge beast, which then dived deep beneath the surface.

Almost immediately, the storm ceased. The dense clouds vanished, and the warm, bright sunlight filled heaven and earth.

As the vision continued, the dreamer was unaware of a minor disturbance downstairs, in the sitting room of the guest house. Some of the guests had been sitting there, chatting and watching television, when the lights flickered, then dimmed, and the television went dead. It fact, the same thing happened in every building within a six-mile radius of Liskeard.

This peculiar inconvenience began almost as soon as Jordan went into his trance, and ended with his return to consciousness. Had he known of it, he might have smiled a faint, enigmatic smile. And if anyone else were to learn the cause of this disturbance, they would have paused, then felt a mixture of fear and awe.

The vision now began to fade, and the sphere's bright light diminished. Soon, it was gone, and the orb resumed its place on the tree whence it had fallen. The tree itself then receded, and vanished.

The vision passed. Barad moved aside, and Eliezer Jordan returned to the fore. As he did, his vital functions resumed their normal rates. His eyelids quivered, then opened. Except for the slight twitching of his nostrils, and the quick movement of his eyes, he was motionless.

"By the baboons of dawn!" he exclaimed, in a whisper. From the tape came the last few bars of Mendelssohn's Fingal's Cave.

Jordan shut the recorder. A long moment later, the puzzled mystic removed his skullcap and prayer shawl and put both into his tote bag. As he did, electrical power was restored as quickly and mysteriously as it had stopped, and everyone in the area viewed the event with some wonder.

Eliezer Jordan, also, wondered. Why did he have this peculiar vision? Why had he seen the prophet Jonah being thrown into the sea, and swallowed by a great fish?

Bewildered, he simply shrugged his shoulders, washed, then went downstairs, and had a simple dinner.

CHAPTER 30

▼

THE GREAT RENEWAL

A brisk, fresh wind blew in from what the English audaciously called "their" channel. Slowly but steadily, it dispersed the ominous clouds that had dominated the heavens for a fortnight.

The sky was clear, and the air quite invigorating, when Alice Penrose's guests left the meeting that she had hosted. They were eager to return home, on this, the wind-swept third Sunday of December. The eve of the winter solstice was fast approaching—a night of great portent would soon be upon them. A great, fearful, ominous time.

It had been viewed as such by peoples around the world for unnumbered centuries. On this awesome day, the sun disappeared, and had to be found, and rekindled. The forces of light and life waned, and had to be renewed—brought back to the world, and to the lives of all earth-bound creatures.

As born-again pagans, Alice Penrose and her friends would engage in the old rituals, and recite the old chants and spells, at the many sacred locations. Wearing medallions etched with strange designs and charms, and flowing robes of soothing colors and hues, their druidic groups would foregather in solemn assembly. They would meet at monuments whose origins were lost in the hoary mists of antiquity.

The members of nearly two hundred druidic circles came out on this cold, clear, star-lit night. They came by car and van, and left their vehicles outside the confines of the hallowed meeting places. The here-and-now was left behind, and the past was summoned and welcomed to fore.

Singly, and by two's and three's, the Keepers of the Ley Lines arrived at the ancient monument at Chysauster. As the last of them arrived, robes, pendants, and headdresses were donned. Solemnly, the worshippers lined up and approached the monument in awe and reverence. They walked with measured steps, each celebrant an arm's length from the next.

Several worshippers, including those at the fore and aft of the two lines, carried pine knot torches, which they held aloft. Every few paces, they waved their lights in strange patterns—as if, by their motions, they could rekindle the sun, and bring its life-sustaining light and warmth back to Earth.

As this was no ordinary ceremony, so were these no ordinary torches. Strange, pungent herbs and spices had been added to them, that by their burning they might fill both the eyes and nostrils of the great and mighty spirits being summoned this night.

Other celebrants carried wicker baskets of various shapes and sizes. Some of the baskets contained fresh, aromatic wreaths of mistletoe. Others held cuttings from the yew, the ash, and other sacred trees and plants. In the middle of this company, one worshipper held a basket whose singular contents were of great importance to the entire assembly.

The three lines of worshippers neared the monolith. As they did, they chanted in an ancient, long-forgotten tongue. When they all stood around it, their funereal chanting halted.

A somber silence now settled over Chysauster, and over the grim assembly. It was just barely broken by the sound of ruffling robes, as some of the celebrants lowered their baskets, or waved their torches.

For several minutes, they continued in this manner, as the rest of the company looked on. Some of them fidgeted, or grimaced, every now and then, either from mild impatience, or in anticipation.

After a brief silence, four torchbearers stepped forward, and stood at the corners of a massive recumbent stone. As they held their torches aloft, their grim-faced leader approached.

In his left hand, he held his druidic staff of office. A bronze cap was affixed to its top. Carved on it were two small heads, facing in opposite directions.

Around his neck he wore a finely designed ceremonial torc. On his right wrist was a wide leather band, on which there was a medallion decorated with the head of an ancient deity.

Malcolm Morgan walked around the monolith with a strong, determined step. Then, he turned around, holding his priestly staff in front of him. Facing the other 'Keepers,' he began to chant in the old Celtic language.

"Forces of Light—Forces of Dark. Come from beyond the nether world."

"We summon Sequanna of the life-giving waters, to cleanse impurities from Albion's soil," the rest of them chanted.

"Mast of Maccha, lead us through perils," the druid continued, as a woman stepped forward with her basket, and its grisly contents, and placed it on the altar.

"Spirits of darkness—do not overwhelm us. Spirits of light, brighten Albion. Let the Sun return from the Land of Enchantments," his filidh, James Woodson, solemnly intoned.

"Lower the dying sun into the cauldron of the Danaan," he said, as two worshippers brought forward a small copper pot.

Ellen Chatham now stepped forward—for once, without her knitting needles. A strong light was in her eyes as she stretched her arms over the massive altar, and began to sway slowly and rhythmically.

"Navel of the Earth, nourish us with light," she prayed.

"Axis of the World, our entreaties are funneled through you. Forces of light—forces of darkness—let thy servants maintain thy balance."

She paused, and the rest of the assembly continued. "Powers above, and powers below—flowing through Albion through secret channels—guide back the sun to the land of your supplicants."

Two of those supplicants now came forward, and stood behind their priestess. They held up the two poles that they had been carrying, and moved apart. They revealed a tanned sheepskin that had been ritually prepared for this purpose.

On it was a rough, hand-drawn map of Europe. The ancient, sacred sites were indicated, in blue. Connecting those sites were lines of bright yellow.

"Lines of power—lines of mystery," Ellen continued. "Nourish thy guardians. Transport our prayers to the netherworld. Safeguard thy land, and thy keepers, on this day of great darkness."

Again, she paused. Three worshippers now stepped forward. and placed their baskets upon the altar. Andrew Barrett then handed a torch to Morgan.

"Powers of light—powers of dark," the druid chanted. "Restore Albion's purity. Preserve its safety, and the safety of these, thy supplicants. Brighten the paths of the ancient days. Let the sacrifice cleanse the land, and stand vigil o'er the sacred ley lines."

One by one, he removed the covers of each basket, revealed their horrid contents. In each was a severed head, preserved in wax and honey.

"O ye severed heads, watch over us," he intoned. "Search for the Light along hidden paths, and point its return to us."

As he ended his prayer, he lowered his torch, and set the three baskets on fire. One by one, they burst into a bright flame, bringing gasps of awe from the robed worshippers.

This bizarre gathering ended two hours later, when the baskets had been reduced to smoking embers. As the flames, and their prayers, ended, some of the worshippers came forward, and cleaned away the dusty remnants of their frightening offering.

The fires of Chysauster died. A welcome silence now ruled, where the sounds of dire incantations had so recently assailed the heavens. Cold and distant, a million twinkling stars looked down. They cast their silvery hue on the spot where a deadly fire had briefly blazed.

The scene now was dark and lovely, the silence moving, now that the last of the worshippers had left. Here and there, a cloud floated across the sky.

Several miles to the southwest, a man sat on a bed in a guesthouse in Liskeard. As another winter's night covered Cornwall, he sat, doodling with a pen and a large pad.

There was a definite purpose to his scribbling. He was working on a puzzle–a puzzle whose picture would shock him, once he learned its meaning.

CHAPTER 31

▼

ENCOURAGEMENT

John Kelly was beaming with enthusiasm as he picked up the phone, and dialed the number of a very special lady. They spoke in hushed, animated tones for a couple of minutes. He appeared excited and optimistic, when he hung up.

Turning to his friends, he flashed a broad smile. In fact, his face was brighter than it had been for some time.

"Well, gentlemen, I'm off," he said, with some enthusiasm. "Where are we going?" asked Hobbs. He sprang up, eager to play an active part in whatever was about to unfold.

John Kelly put a reassuring hand in his friend's shoulder. "Not 'we', I'm afraid," he said, in genuine sorrow. "I am off to visit Mrs. MacFarland—I go alone."

Kelly wrapped himself in his coat and scarf, and put on his hat. He left the office, and took the elevator downstairs. With all due haste, and an unerring sense of purpose, he went directly to his destination.

Hobbs and Ferguson exchanged glances as their friend left them.

"Well, this **is** a blot on our escutcheon, I must say!" the former finally exclaimed.

"A blot? How so?" as the Scot, as he began to fold another sheet of paper.

"Why, the plain and simple fact that one of our own colleagues—a man of Mr. Kelly's probity—should consort with members of the criminal classes."

Sean Ferguson said nothing. He simply went on with his folding. At last, satisfied with what he had done, he smiled, and placed the figure of an ibex on his desk.

Now, he looked at Hobbs. He raised his eyebrows, shook his head, and chuckled.

"I daresay, Hobbs, that between you and Kelly, Thespis is firmly entrenched here at the Yard. He and I are very much aware of the irony, I can assure you," he added, on a serious note. "And we've both often felt quite awkward about it."

Pausing for a moment, he filled and lit his first pipe of the day. "But I've come to know him fairly well," he added. "And I trust him completely. If John Kelly is willing to vouch for the mysterious Mrs. MacFarland, I'm just as willing to accept his word on it."

Hobbs thought for a moment, then shrugged his shoulders in resignation. "Do you think his quest will bear fruit?"

"I certainly hope so," said Ferguson. "Kelly has very good instincts, but even **he** is fallible. I should hate to see him go off on some wild goose chase."

Kelly's partner clenched his pipe between his teeth, then reached into the bottom drawer of his desk. He removed a thick book containing schedules of rail service throughout Britain. He placed on the desk in front of him, and began to thumb through it.

When he found what he wanted, he nodded, and smiled in satisfaction. He then looked at Hobbs and asked, "Are you keen on a railway journey?"

Hobbs leaned forward in eager anticipation.

"A railway journey?" he asked. "Yes—of course. Where are we going?"

Ferguson smiled a quiet, almost sly smile and tapped his nose. "This is very old, very dear friend," he said. "It's often served as—well, as a divining rod, you might say."

"And where does it point, now?" Hobbs almost smiled.

"Towards Bodmin."

"And another meeting with Sgt. Bailey?" Hobbs asked.

"The answers to our problems are out there, somewhere," said Ferguson, with a wave of his arm. "Somewhere, out on the frosty English countryside."

A look of grim determination came to Ferguson's face.

"And then, there's the personal factor," he added, as he began to clean his tobacco-blackened pipe. "Our adversary has killed and mutilated thirteen people. He's successfully eluded us, and made fools of the whole damned lot of us. I want to do whatever I can, to turn the tables on him!"

"Or her," suggested Hobbs. "How may I help you?" asked Hobbs.

Ferguson seemed to ignore the younger man. "It's eleven o'clock, now. I have just enough time to hurry home, toss a few things together, then catch the 2:06 from Paddington."

Hobbs scowled as Ferguson shrugged into his overcoat.

"You're not going alone, are you?" he asked, chagrined. "What am I supposed to do, whilst you're meandering over the moors, and amongst cairns and monoliths?"

Sean Ferguson had just gotten his coat on, when he suddenly paused. Slightly bewildered, he looked at Hobbs.

"'Moors and monoliths'," he breathed. "How odd that you should put it that way. I never really thought of it like that. What made you mention them?"

"It seems only natural," said Hobbs. "After all, you'll be very close to Dartmoor and Bodmin Moor. And as for stone circles well, Cornwall is a veritable museum. You'll find Lanyan Quoit, Trethevy Quoit, and the Hurlers, to name but three. Why?"

A far-away look came to the Scot's face. It stayed there for but a few seconds, as an image came to his mind's eye.

The picture was of a visitor from St.Ives, come to London a few days earlier with a priceless book of old Welsh tales—and of Kelly waxing poetic at the sight of a drawing of five oddly-shaped circles. He shut his eyes tightly, then shook his head, and returned to the matter at hand.

"It just seemed a bit odd, I suppose," he finally said. "It reminded me of something I saw the other day."

"Well, then," Hobbs asked. "Shall I come with you?"

"Have you forgotten?" Ferguson reminded him. "Your 'damsel in distress' is coming back to see you, first thing Monday morning."

"Damn! You're right."

Ferguson smiled sympathetically. "Cheer up, old sport. Something tells me that you'll be joining me, ere long," he said, confidently.

He opened the door, and was about to leave, when he paused. "Please tell Kelly where I've gone. If an American named Jordan should ring, take any messages and forward them. It's most urgent."

"Very well," said Hobbs, in a tone of some resignation. "I hope you know what you're doing."

"So do I, Hobbs. So do I," said the Scot, as he closed the door, and hurried off.

CHAPTER 32

▼

CURIOSITY

Eliezer Jordan had finished supper. He spent a pleasant hour strolling leisurely about Liskeard. He enjoyed the crisp winter's evening, so different from New Jersey. He returned to the guesthouse a few minutes before nine, and dialed a number in London.

On the fourth ring, Peggy Ferguson answered. Her rich voice was unmistakable.

"Oh! Hello, Eli. Sean left early this afternoon. I found a note from him. He's going to Bodmin."

Jordan tugged his lower lip pensively. "That's unexpected news," he said. "Well, if he should call—or if you could contact Insp. Kelly—ask them to learn what they can about something called 'Festival of the Deermen.' It's held at Abbott's Bromley. Good. Thanks. Yes, I'll be careful," he promised, then hung up.

Several other guests were already in the sitting room when Jordan entered. He picked up a newspaper from a neatly polished table, and found a quiet corner in which to read the day's news. He was paying only partial attention when the local news broadcast came over the television.

He perked up a bit when mention was made of the evening's brief power failure. He was amused to hear that people had phoned the studio, and offered quite an assortment of 'explanations' for the event: playful pixies; disturbed earth-currents; the coming winter solstice; America's space program; and demonic forces let loose at Samhuin, the ancient forerunner of Hallowe'en.

Jordan smiled slightly. What would people think if he were to reveal the real cause? he wondered. He sighed. Then, with a shrug of his shoulders, he closed his paper, put it on the table, and retired for the evening.

Ever the early riser, Jordan awoke shortly after dawn the next morning. It was the winter solstice, according to the calendar hanging on the door of his room.

He washed and dressed, then spent some time in meditation. Renewed and refreshed, he went downstairs with his map, and pad and pen in hand. Breakfast was pleasant, and the portions generous, though he ate sparingly as was his custom. As he finished, he gazed out the window.

The pale winter sunlight brightened Liskeard with an eerie light. A long, narrow rainbow was just barely visible, high in the heavens, as the stark sunlight filtered through the moist sky.

Something strange—something mysterious and intangible—permeated the atmosphere on this, the day of the winter solstice. Jordan didn't notice it at first, but he did sense the tense silence in which the other guests entered, and ate their meals. He would see it again, later, when he went outside, and walked through town.

"This is spooky," he thought. "Like some funereal calm before an awesome storm. I wonder what it is."

Bewildered, he shook his head. Then, he opened his map, and studied it. Slowly, he traced a line with his pen. One by one, he stopped at the sites of each killing.

"Hmm—that's odd," he noted, when his hand finally came to a halt. "Odd, and interesting. The first murder was in Bodmin, on September 5. Now, tracing the sequence, the line returns to Bodmin.

Excited, he rechecked the dates and sites of the murders. Three times, his eyes shifted back and forth between the list and the map. Once again, his index finger glided over the line that he had drawn. Again, he began at Bodmin, moving in an ellipse until he reached Hadrian's Wall. Then, he moved directly south, to London, before stopping where he had begun.

A smile of satisfaction came to his face. "Ah," he thought. "Finally—a pattern seems to be emerging."

A few minutes later, his face lit up again. "Ahh—here's something else," he said, as he tapped each site with his finger. "Odd—very odd. I should contact Ferguson and Kelly, and tell them what I've found."

Quickly, he folded up his map, and looked at his watch. "Hmm. 8:20. I'd better get moving. There's a lot to be done, and I still don't have a plan of action."

Jordan retrieved his coat and scarf, then went outside. He took a long walk about the town because something nagged him—something that he could not quite define.

"Damn! It's so damn tantalizing," he grumbled. "Ferguson suspected that there was some method to this madness. Now, I seem to have found two patterns. Do they signify anything?"

He shook his head, and grimaced. Then, he quietly laughed at his impatience.

"After all, I've been here only three days. At least I've made some headway," he reminded himself.

He retraced his steps. As he walked, he could not fail to notice the uneasy, almost unearthly silence around him. There was an air of apprehension that could almost be touched, even if it couldn't be explained.

Jordan noticed it. He was curious to know its cause. As he got into his car, he made a mental note to ask someone about it.

CHAPTER 33

▼

HEADS AND TAILS

For the third time in three days, Jordan headed for Bodmin. As he drove, two men were having a polite difference of opinion in Bodmin's police station.

Reginald Bailey leaned against the side of his desk, his hands loosely clasped over his midsection. His face wore a look of polite skepticism. "I don't mean to be rude," he was saying. "But aren't you wasting your time?"

"You really think so?" asked Sean Ferguson, who sat there, toying with his ever-present briar pipe.

Bailey replied with a firm nod. "Let's suppose that the same chap is behind these murders," he said.

"Or woman," Ferguson suggested.

"How's that?"

"Or woman," the Scot repeated. "I was simply thinking that our elusive quarry could be a woman. Or a man and a woman, acting together."

"It's possible, or course. But how likely is it? I can see a woman using poison, or a dagger between the ribs. But now? I sense a man's mind and hand in this. Not a woman's." He stood up, and poured some cocoa for himself and his visitor.

"That's a moot question just now, I think," he continued. "It doesn't explain what brings you here again. Not checking up on us provincials, are you?" Bailey asked, with a wry smile.

"Oh, no—of course not," replied the Scot, sharing that smile. "If anything, it's I who need the check-up. Kelly and I have been stymied for three-and-a-half months—it's devilishly frustrating!" he remarked.

Exasperated, he stood up, and stretched his limbs. "Something you mentioned yesterday brings me here," he then said.

Bailey's face registered a look of mild surprise, as Ferguson opened his note-pad.

"Let me see. This was-Number 13? Yes-the thirteenth so far," Ferguson observed, as he checked his notes. "Four bodies were found in or next to churches-two of them right here in Bodmin. Six bodies each bore a small tattoo two were of spotted serpents."

"So? You could have told me that yesterday, on the phone."

"Perhaps. Tell me something-do think it's merely a coincidence?"

"Yes, I do. Now, look here, Inspector," said Bailey, gesturing with his left hand for emphasis. "As I see it, there are always two ways of looking at things-heads, or tails. Heads-four bodies were found in or near churches. Tails-nine weren't. Heads-six victims had tattoos. Tails-seven didn't."

Momentarily checked, Ferguson said and did nothing. Obviously discouraged by Bailey's skepticism, he drew a deep breath, and let it out slowly. Then, the tip of his nose twitched, and a trace of a smile came to his face.

"What can you tell me about Maidenwell?" he asked, apparently changing the subject.

"Maidenwell? There's very little **to** tell. I told everything to Hobbs, on the phone, yesterday. Why?" Bailey asked, a bit annoyed.

"I was thinking of a curious coincidence. The young woman whose death started this tragedy-her name was Jocelyn Miller. She lived in

Maidenwell, didn't she?" Fer-guson asked, checking his notes. "And the fellow who was killed on Friday-he lived in Helland," he recalled.

Bailey gave him a questioning look. "That's right," he said. "What of it? So do several other people. What are you driving at?"

"A set of strange coincidences. There's a pattern here, Sergeant. I'm sure of it. But we won't find it-or the murderer-if we start fighting amongst ourselves."

"I suppose you're right. Very well-let's look at these 'coincidences', if only for the sake of argument. What do they mean? Where do they lead us?"

"Perhaps I can answer that," a new voice suggested, before the Scot could reply.

The two policemen turned. They saw a sturdy figure standing in the doorway. He wore a warm, friendly smile on his chilled face, while they wore looks of surprise on theirs.

CHAPTER 34

▼

PATTERNS

Sean Ferguson stepped forward, and eagerly greeted his friend.

"Eli—what are you doing here?"

"You did ask for my help. Remember? I rang you in London last night. Peggy told me that you were here."

"Come in, won't you? Sergeant, this is a good friend, Prof. Eli Jordan. Eli, this is Sgt. Bailey, of the Bodmin police," said the Scot.

"We've met," said Jordan, as he and the Cornishman shook hands.

Jordan wasted no time. He took out his map and opened it on Bailey's desk.

"Gentlemen, I've learned a few things that might interest you," he said. "Last night, I discovered some patterns to these killings. First-their locations form an irregular triangle, with Bodmin, London, and an ancient Roman fort along Hadrian's Wall as its corners.

"Second-the first ten murders follow a line of sorts. They began in Bodmin on September 5, and reached the Wall with two more on October 28, with seven gruesome stops along the way.

"Third-the first eight were concentrated in the southwest of England, between Bodmin and Chipping-Norton.

There were none between Chipping-Norton and the Wall; none between the Wall and London; and none between London and Bodmin."

"Fourth-this deadly triangle begins, and ends-thus far, at least-right here in Bodmin."

Bailey fidgeted a bit. "Tell me something, Professor," he asked. "You're not a policeman-what's your interest in this case?"

"Jordan helped us solve that affair at Tintagel, two years ago," Ferguson explained. "I asked him to come here, as a personal favor."

Jordan continued. "Friday afternoon, I came here, to visit the church-just in time to see that another murder had been committed. I spoke with Mr. Thomson a short while later, and again yesterday morning. It was good that I returned, for a few rather peculiar, almost bizarre, things turned up."

Jordan revealed his second conversation with Rev. Thomson. The policemen listened as he shared his findings. When he finished, Bailey chewed his lip, then grudgingly apologized.

"Sorry, Insp. Ferguson," he said. "So, there **is** a spotted serpent involved in this."

He shook his head. "Banshees? Balor? Cernunnos? Who'd have thought it?"

"Do these characters mean anything to you, Sergeant?" Jordan asked.

"As a Cornishman? Most certainly," he said, as he echoed the sentiments that Rev. Thomson had voiced the previous morning.

"My compliments," Ferguson congratulated his friend. "I must say that you haven't wasted any time or energy."

"Thanks. Let's chalk it up to good luck-I was lucky enough to be in the right place at the right time," Jordan smiled.

"True enough. But these patterns—they've been right in front of us, all along. And we never noticed them."

"Neither did I, at first. All of us usually fail to notice the obvious. Do you remember Poe's short story, 'The Purloined Letter'? The best place to hide something is often in plain sight."

"Well, gentlemen?" Bailey now asked them. "What are we to make of all this? Where does it lead us?"

"It leads me to the assumption that there's a connection between the murders, and these mythological characters," said Jordan. "Of course, it remains to be seen if a connection does exist and, if so, what it might be."

"I see your point," said Bailey. He knitted his brow, thought for a minute, then, "I think that I'll call on Rev. Thomson. I should like to see those drawings for myself."

"I'd like to come along, if you don't mind," Ferguson politely asked. "By the way, have you visited the family of the fellow who was killed on Friday?"

"Only very briefly, last evening. I thought it best to wait until after the funeral, before I asked any questions. Why?"

"I'd like to join you, if you've no objections. And I think that another visit to the family of the unfortunate Miss Miller is in order."

"A good idea," Bailey agreed. "See if they may have known each other, or had any mutual acquaintances."

"And see if either ever showed an interest in Celtic lore-or in the figures on those sketches," the Scot added.

"Let's get on it straightaway, then," said Bailey, as he got up, and reached for his coat.

"What about you, Professor? What do you plan to do, now?" he then asked.

"I haven't decided yet. There are a couple of things I'd like to look into. I may move on, tomorrow morning," Jordan replied. He turned to leave, then paused. "By the way, has either of you ever heard of the 'Festival of the Deer-Men'?" he asked.

"No. What is it?"

"Mr. Thomson mentioned it, as a possible hold-over from the worship of Cernunnos. It's held in Abbotts-Bromley on September 4. And the murders began on the fifth. Or rather, the first body was found on the fifth," said Jordan. "It may be a coincidence, but I think that it's worth looking into," he suggested. Then, with a firm nod, he departed.

CHAPTER 35

▼

DESPAIR AND HOPE

The afternoon was almost gone when John Kelly, cold and tired, entered Insp. Hobbs' office.

"Mr. Kelly—how was your search?" Hobbs inquired. "Fruitless."

Kelly slumped into a chair and ran his fingers through his hair. "I've just been studying an encyclopedia of tattoos. Nearly three thousand designs, arranged and cross-referenced by category and place of origin. And not a single spotted serpent in the whole damned lot!"

He cursed his unknown adversary, and slapped the arm of the chair with a force that one would not expect from one of his lean build.

That simple act helped to dissipate some of his anger. Then, in a calmer tone, he asked, "Where's Ferguson?"

"Bodmin."

"Bodmin? Why?"

"To Bodmin? What ever for? Has something happened?"

"He merely said something about 'professional instincts.' A hunch, I believe the Americans call it."

For the first time in quite a while, Kelly smiled. "Thanks, Hobbs," he said. "Bodmin. Hmm. Jordan was there. Now, Ferguson. The murder on Friday. The girl who came to you for help. Maybe Ferguson's on to something."

"I certainly hope so," said Hobbs.

Kelly looked at his younger colleague. "No other messages?" he asked.

"None."

"In that case, I'll call it a day," said Kelly. He turned to leave when Hobbs stopped him with a question.

"You'll be here Monday, won't you? My 'damsel in distress' is returning then. I really would appreciate your help."

"A second opinion, eh?" asked Kelly, in a friendly tone. "Very well, Hobbs. I'll be there. Good night."

With a warm parting salute, he turned and left. Retrieving his coat from his office, he returned to the flat that he called home.

Sunday morning. John Kelly had finishing cleaning his flat. He was about to relax with his handcrafted mandolin when the phone rang.

"Yes? Kelly here."

"Ah-good," said a familiar voice.

Kelly became animated at the sound of his friend's voice.

"Ferguson? Where are you?"

"In Bodmin. Jordan came up with something. How soon can you get here?"

"Is it urgent? I promised Hobbs I'd meet that woman."

"The one who went to Bailey about the Woodsons?"

"The same."

There was a long silence, then, "You'd better see her. Strange doings going on here. Ask her about spotted snakes and-". Ferguson reeled off the present facts to his partner.

"Very good," said Kelly. "I'll find out what can about this 'Festival of the Deer-Men.' And I'll come out there as soon as I can."

"Fine. In the meantime, Bailey and I want to follow some leads here. Good-bye."

CHAPTER 36

▼

EXASPERATION

Clovis Hobbs was annoyed when John Kelly failed to report for duty first thing Monday morning. While he anxiously awaited both Kelly and Miss Miller, the former was at his local public library. For two hours, he went through several books with an enthusiasm that he had not felt for some time. At last, satisfied with what he had found, he eagerly hurried to his office.

He was in fine spirits when he entered Scotland Yard. His mood didn't sour even when Chief Inspector Oswald crossed his path.

"Where have you been, Kelly?! You're late!" Oswald snapped, pointing to a clock on the wall.

"And the moon is made of cheddar cheese," came the quick retort. "Actually. I've been at my neighbourhood library, reading about Abbott's Bromley."

Kelly grinned. "It's amazing, isn't it? What a colorful assortment of facts one might find within a library's walls."

"Is that how you and Ferguson waste public funds?"

"My, my. Aren't we chipper today?"

Kelly entered the lift without waiting for a reply. Arriving at his floor, Kelly went directly to Hobbs' office.

An air of tension filled the tidy room, as Hobbs and a young woman faced each other across the detective's desk.

"Sorry I'm late," Kelly apologized to his beleaguered friend.

"Very well," said Hobbs. "This is Miss Miller, the woman I told you about. Miss Miller-my colleague, Insp. Kelly."

John Kelly nodded, then walked to the window and leaned against the sill.

"Gwen is in trouble-I know it," the distraught woman insisted. "We must go to Maidenwell and help her."

"I've told Miss Miller of our call to Sgt. Bailey," Hobbs told Kelly. "She refuses to believe that we see nothing worth investigating and that legally, there is naught that we can do for her."

Kelly frowned. "One of our colleagues is presently in Bodmin," he told her. "He and Sgt. Bailey are working on another case. But I don't see how we can help you. Are we to remove your one-time friend forcibly from her home? Because she refuses to meet or speak with you? Your pride has been wounded, Miss Miller-that is all," he said, with a note of finality in his voice.

"All?! How can you say that?! Oh, you men are all alike-mentally myopic-emotionally calcified!" she berated them.

"And you, Miss Miller, are acting just like a woman," was Kelly's quick retort. "You're hysterical and irrational. Your wounded pride blinds you the obvious—Mrs. Woodson no longer desires your friendship. She has committed no other 'crime.'"

"Nor broken any law," Hobbs added. "Which is why we are powerless to help. I'm sorry."

His words fell on deaf ears. Miss Miller got up. Her eyes blazed with anger as she stared intently at the two men.

"Very well," she said, in a harsh whisper. "Since you refuse to help, I will do what I can, on my own. Good day."

CHAPTER 37

▼

DREAD AND FORBODING

Eliezer Jordan emerged from the Bodmin police station. He was pleased that he had learned so much in only three days, and had been of some help to his friend. Just the same, he felt that his involvement in the case had only just begun-that much more remained to be done before it was brought to a close.

Then he heard his stomach grumble-a reminder that he had not eaten since six the previous evening. He soon found a pub just off the town's main thoroughfare. He entered, went to a table nestled in a corner, and ordered a simple meal.

The atmosphere of tension-of nervous anticipation-that he had noticed earlier in the day was more obvious, now. He barely touched his food as he sat there, studying his surroundings. What was amiss?

Curiosity prompted Jordan to walk to the bar. "Excuse me," he asked the bartender. "Everyone seems to edgy-so apprehensive. What is it?"

The man eyed the stranger warily. "You're a foreigner, aren't you? A Yank?" he asked, as he tried to size up the newcomer. Jordan nodded.

"Today is the winter solstice," his informant told him. "The day with the fewest hours of light, and most of darkness."

"Yes, I know. But what's the connection? The anxiety seems thick enough to touch."

"It's plain you're not a Cornishman-otherwise, you'd know the reason."

"Well, could you satisfy my curiosity?" Jordan politely repeated.

The lowered his voice to a subdued tone. "The ancient ways die hard, here in Cornwall. In some places, they're still very much alive. Three months ago, a series of murders began, each in another part of England. Three were in churchyards-two here in Bodmin, and one in Glastonbury." He paused.

For a minute or to, he seemed reluctant to go on. Even after four months, the memory of those crimes still lived in the minds of these people.

"And three were committed near the end of October, just before All Hallows," said another man, who heard Jordan's questions.

"All Hallows? That's Halloween, isn't it?"

"It is," said the second man.

"It has an unpleasant connotation, judging from the tone of your voice, and that look on your face," Jordan deduced.

"Have you ever heard of Samhuin?" the bartender asked Jordan. "It was an ancient Celtic festival held once each year, on the last night of October. A night of dread and foreboding-when the forces of evil threatened to overrun the world."

"It sounds like Walpergistnacht," said Jordan.

"Too much like it," said another, in a tone of awe and dread.

"Well, I'm beginning to see-a little," said Jordan. "But how does the winter solstice fit in?"

"It's a day that's been feared and revered since time began. It was second only to Samhuin as a day of awe, and of dire premonitions. The forces of darkness had to be warded off, and the power of the sun renewed-by magic, and by sacrifices-usually of cattle, though sometimes of humans as well." The speaker took a long, deep drink of ale.

"Thank you, gentlemen, for satisfying a visitor's curiosity," he told them. "It's a strange tale, but it does explain the subdued atmosphere."

A light suddenly came to his eyes, followed by a hearty smile. His nimble mind made an intuitive connection. He paid his bill, then went outside to his car.

CHAPTER 38

▼

THE PRIMORDIAL WATERS

Another cold night descended upon Britain. Jordan sat silently on his bed at the guesthouse. He wore a blue terry-cloth robe, as he sat with a writing pad on his lap.

His pencil went across the pad, dividing the paper into several squares. In each square, he wrote one of the facts that he had learned, since his arrival in England. Then, he separated the squares, and placed them on the bed.

Silently and deliberately, he studied these pieces of a mysterious and deadly puzzle. Every few minutes, he moved the paper scraps around, to form a new pattern. Now and then, he rubbed his chin, or grimaced, as he tried to make some sense of it all.

What could it be? Thirteen murders-started in Bodmin, on September 5. Back in Bodmin, on December20. Each body mutilated in some way-usually amputation, or decapitation. Always a clean wound-implying the skilled hand of a surgeon.

Jordan leaned over slightly, and let his gaze wander over the squares. "Most of the murders were between Bodmin and Chipping-Norton, then nothing until Hadrian's Wall. Most were in one area, with three large gaps-Chipping-Norton to the Wall, then down to London, and back to Bodmin. I wonder if it means anything. Let me see-what did Ferguson say? Yes-two bodies were found at an old Roman fort at Brocolitia. That name rings a bell."

His face lit up. "Of course. It has a Mithraic temple."

He shifted his position, and shook his head, in an effort to stay awake. "Balor-Cernunnos-Banshees. Now, Mithra. Oh, boy-we really have a nice bag of goods on our hands," he thought, as he scratched his head.

Unable to stay awake any longer, he scooped up the paper squares and put them into the pocket of his robe. Removing the robe, he got into bed, and fell quickly asleep.

For most of the night, it was a light, peaceful sleep. Then, as the first pale streaks of dawn crawled over the eastern horizon, he slipped into a deep, heavy sleep.

Mind and body were both soon in a state of total relaxation, and heightened sensitivity. The sleeper felt himself transported across time and space, as though neither had any hold on him.

At last, his astral journey came to a halt. Immediately, he recognized the site-it was the fertile landscape near Dendereh, in Upper Egypt, where barren desert and lush, cultivated land stood in sharp contrast to each other.

In his mind's eye he saw the Island of Creation, as pictured in the ancient Egyptian creation myth. The place where it all began. The island on which Atum, the primordial creator, had come forth from Nun, the primeval waters, and produced Shu, god of the air, and Tefnut, goddess of moisture.

One image stood out, pre-eminent over all the others. It was Nun, the ancient cosmic waters from which all else had emerged. The vision was a brief one. It lasted only long enough for the sleeper to become aware of it. Then, it receded, back into the vast cosmic abyss from whence it had come.

So, too, did the soul of the sleeper speed across the cosmos, returning to the dormant body in which it dwelled. Slowly, reluctantly, Eliezer Jordan began to awaken. He looked and felt like one who was coming out of a deep hypnotic trance, or from a strong anaesthetic.

Slowly, he sat up. Still partly asleep, he shifted his legs around, and lowered his feet to the floor. He groaned, rubbed his face, and slowly returned to total consciousness.

"What the hell is going on? Nothing common-place, I'm sure of that," he muttered, as he stood up, then washed and dressed.

"First, those dreams of a weathered stone pillar. Then, Jonah being swallowed by a huge fish. Now, the Egyptian creation myth."

Standing by the sink, his face still wet, he studied his face in the mirror. "Jonah, on his way to Nineveh. An old stone pillar, with blood oozing from a faceless head. Now, Nun, the primordial waters of creation."

He shook his head, then dried his face. Returning to the bed, he packed his tote-bag. A couple of times he paused and muttered to himself. When he finished, he looked around. Satisfied that he had forgotten nothing, he turned, and left.

As he did, he smiled. "Three different dreams—three very different symbols. Answers? Or new questions?"

After a quick breakfast, he checked out, returned the car to the rental agency, then walked to the railway station. His train soon arrived, and took him as far as Exeter. There, he made the first of several changes that would bring him to Hexham late the following afternoon.

What was he seeking? What did he expect to find?

As Jordan made his was to Hexham, two men left the Bodmin police station, got into a car, and drove to Maidenwell.

CHAPTER 39

▼

THE FOUR FESTIVALS

Bailey and Ferguson drove on in an uneasy silence. Bailey slowed down as they approached Maidenwell. He parked the car, and got out. Followed closely by his companion, he walked towards a well-kept cottage. A neat gravel path led from the road to the cottage. On both sides of the path, a well-tended garden sat in snow-covered slumber.

The men paused by the gate. After a moment's pause, Bailey opened it; he and his partner walked up to the cottage, and he knocked on the door.

A woman in her forties soon answered his knock. Crow's feet lined the corners of her dark green eyes, and added something to her strong, weather-beaten appearance.

"Oh—Sgt. Bailey," she said, as she dried her hands on her apron, and invited the callers inside the foyer.

"Yes, ma'am. I'm afraid so," he replied. "This is Inspector Ferguson, of Scotland Yard. I'm afraid that we must ask you and your husband a few questions."

"It's been almost four months. What can you hope to learn now?" she asked.

"We know what you've been through," a sympathetic Ferguson tried to assure her. "We're doing all in our power to track down your daughter's killer."

A man came from the back. His voice was husky with anger and bitterness as he asked, "And where has it gotten you?" a husky voice asked, in an angry, bitter tone. They turned, and saw the father of the murdered girl.

Bailey shuffled his fell uncomfortably.

Husband and wife stood there, defensively. They looked at each other, then at their visitors.

Ferguson broke the uneasy silence. "May we ask you a few questions?" he asked. "It's most important."

"Very well," they grudgingly agreed. "If you think it will do any good."

Bailey drew a long deep breath, and tightened his lips before speaking. "Had your daughter ever shown an interest in the old religion?" he asked.

Mr. Williams narrowed his eyes, cautious. "What has the old religion to do with her death?"

Ferguson cleared his throat. "We've found some evidence to link two of these crimes to each other, and to the ancient Celtic religion," he replied.

"Evidence? What sort of evidence?" Mrs. Williams asked.

The Scot told them of the tattoos borne by some of the victims, and of the ominous sketches received by the vicar.

"Heaven help us," said Mrs. Williams, in a worried whisper. "Who would have imagined?" The woman turned away, moving into the sitting room. Her husband, less antagonistic now, motioned for the police officers to enter.

Ferguson and Bailey stood on the worn braid carpet as Mrs. Williams sat down. Her voice was ghostly quiet as she spoke.

"When the children were young, I used to tell them stories of Arthur," she began. "Oh, they loved to hear the MABINOGION read. Our copy is an heirloom; it's been in my family for several generations."

The woman's pride was dampened by painful memories.

Mr. Williams placed a comforting hand on his wife's shoulder.

"Jo was the only one to show any affinity with the old heritage," he added. "As she grew up, she learned Gaelic. She was interested in the lore of our forefathers. She loved the old ballads, and learned quite a few of them." The man choked back his emotion.

The couple's pain was awful, but Sean Ferguson knew that the best way was to forge ahead.

"Is there anything else you can tell us?" he asked. "What of her friends? Did any of them share her interests?"

Mr. Williams shrugged, but his wife said, "Oh, yes. There were a few here in Maidenwell, and some from Helland, Liskeard, and Cardinham. They met periodically, usually at each other's homes, to share the old tales, and poetry. Some of her friends were like Jo-of an artistic, or somewhat mystical nature. They wanted to preserve the language, and the rich folklore."

Her husband was less than enthusiastic when he said, "But for others, this wasn't enough."

Ferguson and Bailey listened in patient silence. The former finally prompted a continuation with a quizzical raise of his eyebrows.

"We've always been God-fearing people," Williams said. "And our children have never given us cause to be ashamed of them."

Bailey knew that. He had seen the family a few times at Mr. Thompson's church. And during his initial investigation, three months earlier, their neighbors had spoken of them with respect, affection, and kindness.

"But some of the others…" he said, as his voice trailed off.

"Yes, Mr. Williams? What about them?" Bailey wondered.

"They had no fear of God in them, sir. None at all," he said, with some trepidation.

"I'm not one to speak ill of my neighbors, or to traffic in idle gossip," he insisted. "But some of Jo's acquaintances turned their backs on God—they returned to paganism, and the worship of the old gods," he told them, clearly annoyed and upset.

"Really?" asked Bailey. "I've heard of some people wearing robes, and peculiar medallions, and marching somberly around Stonehenge once or twice a year. But I never took them seriously."

"Neither have I," Ferguson added. "A friend of mine has met a few of them. They seem quite harmless and eccentric."

"Humph!" Mr. Williams angrily snorted. "Harmless? Delightful? Not the ones our Jo encountered."

The woman's long-time dissatisfaction with some of her daughter's acquaintances was apparent as she spoke. "Vain and godless creatures they were," she said. "Jo told us that they worshipped the old gods, and marked the four ancient festivals."

The word interested Ferguson. "Four festivals? What are they?" he asked.

The woman looked to her husband, who muttered, "Obviously not a Cornishman."

"No, sir," the detective replied. "Just a policeman, with a difficult job to do."

"There were four festivals marked by our people of old," Mr. Williams began. "Imbolc, held on 1 February, honored Brigit, the potent fertility goddess. Beltane, on 1 May, honored Belenus, the 'shining one.' The Druids drove cattle between two great fires, to protect them against disease, and as a symbolic offering to the sun.

"The feast of Samhuin was held on 1 November. The preceding night was the most important part of the festival, marking the end of one year, and the start of the next."

"Samhuin was devoted to the fertility of the earth and its inhabitants," her husband continued. "The people believed that In Dagda, 'the good god,' insured fertility by uniting with the goddess Morrigan, known as the 'spectre queen,' and 'queen of demons.'"

There was a brief pause. Then, "Why do you want to know all this?" Mrs. Williams asked. "Why is it so important? What does it have to do with Jo's death?"

"We're investigating any aspect that might lead to the murderer's apprehension," was all that Bailey would say.

When she realized that neither officer would say any more than that, she sighed.

"You might speak with some of Jo's friends-people who shared her interests," she suggested. She then gave them the names and addresses of four of her daughter's friends.

Husband and wife then terminated the interview by showing the policemen to the door.

"There's a couple here who can tell you more than we've been able to," said Mr. Williams added, as Bailey opened the door. "In fact, they invited Jo to join them at the festival of Lugnasad, last August."

"Really? Who are they?" asked Bailey.

"James and Gwen Woodson. They live about a mile up the road."

Bailey and Ferguson thanked them for their help, bade them farewell, and left. As they walked to their car, they tried to overcome the feeling caused by this unpleasant duty.

"This is the one part of the job that upsets me the most," said Ferguson. "Getting people to relive their pain and sorrow. By the way, Sergeant, I noticed your reaction when Mrs. Williams mentioned that gathering in August. Does it ring a bell?"

Bailey curled the ends of his mustache. "It does," he replied, with a sense of keen anticipation. "Do you recall that distraught woman who told Hobbs and myself of her visit to her onetime friend?"

"Yes. In fact, she's returning to the Yard Monday morning. Poor Mr. Hobbs," he reflected, with a sympathetic smile.

"Did you ever learn her friend's name?"

"No. Why? What was it?"

"It was Gwen Woodson," Bailey replied.

CHAPTER 40

▼

CAUSE FOR CONCERN

Alice and Malcolm Morgan had just sat down to dinner when the phone rang.

Faintly annoyed, the woman answered it. "Yes? Oh-Jim. No, just starting dinner. Yes, he's here. Of course."

The woman held her hand over the mouthpiece. "It's Jim Woodson," she told her husband. "He wants to speak with you. He sounds upset."

Morgan took the phone. "Jim? Couldn't it wait until after dinner?"

The easy banter turned to silence at Woodson's urgent reply. "The police were here again. This afternoon. They asked about the Williams girl. And about the four festivals."

"Is that all?" asked Morgan, rather dryly.

"Isn't that enough? Besides, my two 'visitors' were Sgt.

Bailey from Bodmin and Insp. Ferguson, of Scotland Yard!"

Morgan's confidence was high when he replied, "Ferguson and Kelly have been on the case from the outset. They've uncovered nothing, and it's unlikely that that will change."

"Well, they may be on to something now," Woodson warned him. The caller sounded worried and distraught as he spoke.

"Calm down, Jim," said Morgan. "I've heard from a well-placed friend that they're as far from a solution as they've ever been."

"What a pity you weren't today-with your 'friend,'" Woodson growled, as he recounted the visit from the two policemen.

Morgan began to appreciate the caller's concern. "I see," he said. "Perhaps it does give us good cause to be wary, but I see no need to act rashly."

"What do you suggest? What should we do?"

"For the time being, nothing."

"Nothing? Why?"

"Listen, Jim. A policeman is like a hound, or a village gossip," Morgan noted, with cynical contempt. "Always sticking his nose into other people's business, poking and probing, until he thinks he has a scent. I don't want to give them that scent. A policeman, like a hound, knows if you're nervous or frightened. Keep your head and nothing can go wrong. Just the same, I'm glad you rang," he said. "After all, forewarned is forearmed."

With that, Morgan terminated the call. He stood by the phone, wondering why the police gone to see Woodson twice in four days. Had they learned anything? Or were they merely sniffing around?

Frowning, he returned to the table and finished his meal. "What is it?" his wife asked.

"The police were at the Woodsons' again," he said, then summarized what he had just heard.

His wife twisted the napkin in her lap. "What can we do?" she asked, anxiously.

"Wait and watch," he advised. "Do nothing precipitous."

With an abrupt nod, she agreed. "Any rash act on our part could give them just the clues they need."

Morgan lit a cigarette, then toyed with it. "The police are baffled," he said. "They're stupid and blundering. We'll be safe as long as we do nothing to equal their stupidity. As long as we do nothing foolish, the police can't possibly suspect anything."

He stared at the glowing coals in the fireplace, thinking intently.

"How will this affect our plans for the Druids' Council?" she asked, as they cleared the table.

"Not at all, I hope," he replied, cautiously optimistic. "We've been very lucky thus far," said his wife. "Who would suspect that our faith is as widespread and growing as it is?"

Her face beamed enthusiastically, as she took and lit one of her husband's cigarettes.

"Hopefully, no one suspects. I want to keep it that way. That's why we'll go ahead with our plans-calmly, quietly, steadily."

With that, they put aside all thoughts of the police, and of thirteen gruesome ritual murders. Now, they had a far more pleasant activity to pursue-the beginning of a tapestry depicting the mythological Battle of Mag Tured, the fierce encounter between the Tuatha de Danaan, the 'People of the Goddess Danu,' and the Fomoire, a fearsome race of aboriginal giants.

They worked for two hours, in an enviable harmony and peace of mind. Then, suddenly, the woman tensed, and a look of anxiety came over her face. "What is it, Alice?" her husband asked, nervously.

"I sense danger," she replied, in a husky whisper.

"Danger? What is it? Where is it coming from?"

There was a heavy silence. She began to breathe slowly and deeply. "A man is going north, to meet Mithra. He is looking for us; if he finds us, there will be a deadly reckoning," was all she could say.

"Who is he?" the man asked.

"I don't know. All I can see is an image of a hailstone."

CHAPTER 41

▼

"WE CAN'T AFFORD TO DAWDLE!"

"Mr. Hobbs, why can't a woman be more like a man?" asked
Kelly, after Janet Miller left the office in a thoroughly feminine huff.

Clovis Hobbs looked askance at his colleague. "Good Lord, sir! How
can you say such a thing? Snicker if you must, but I thank the gods that
women are so-well, so delightfully womanly."

Ever the misogynist, John Kelly did snicker. Then, he shook his head.
"I'm certain that she'll not get very far," he finally said.

"You have a point," Hobbs agreed. "The poor, frail maid-meandering,
confused and alone, amidst moors and monoliths-enveloped by the chilling embrace of Albion's shroud-like mists."

Any comment that Kelly might have made just then was cut short by
the ringing of the phone. His colleague answered it. "Hobbs here. How
may I help you?"

"By finding Kelly, and your 'damsel in distress,'" the caller firmly
replied.

"Ferguson? Any news?"

The Scot growled. "Let me speak with Kelly first."

Hobbs thrust the phone towards Kelly. "He sounds awfully agitated," he warned. "Tread prudently."

Kelly smiled at Hobbs, knowing how abrupt his partner could be. He took the phone, and said, "Yes? Ferguson? What is it?"

"Some progress, albeit minimal," was the fatigued yet satisfied response. "We've found a common thread-Celtic mythology."

Kelly sat up with a start. "No! Really?! Amazing. How did you find it?"

Briefly, Ferguson told him. Then, "Where is Hobbs' frantic young lady?" he asked. "Have you met her yet?"

"Yes. In fact, she left here not three minutes ago," Kelly replied, as he told him what happened.

"Go after her! You must not let her come out here. I fear for her life, if she acts rashly."

"Stop her? How?"

"You'll find a way. One more thing. Be prepared to meet me here in a day or two. Ask Hobbs to join you. Good."

With that, the call ended. And John Kelly's lean face was beaming for the first time in many weeks.

"Well? What is it?" Hobbs wondered, when he saw the change in Kelly's demeanor.

"A lead," Kelly replied, with enthusiasm. "We must contact Miss Miller. You ring her at home-I'll try her at work. She did leave that number, I hope."

Hobbs nodded, jotted down the number, and handed it to him. "Very good," said Kelly. "If you get her, tell her to return here immediately. She must not to venture to Maidenwell!"

"Yes, of course. But what shall I tell her?"

John Kelly stood poised at the door, like an arrow pulled back against a bowstring. "We've just gotten some news. We must share it with her in person."

So saying, he bounded out of the room, and went to his own office with a quick step. Both men made their calls, but could not reach the woman.

"Very well," Kelly told the clerk at her office who answered his call. "Tell her come to the Yard, to see Insp. Hobbs and myself. Without a moment's delay! It's imperative!"

He put the phone down, but continued to hold it firmly with his left hand. The fingers of his right hand began to tap his desk nervously.

"Poxied luck!" he fumed, in angry disappointment. "But wait! She left here but ten minutes ago-she hasn't had time to reach her place of work."

He sat back, and heaved a sigh of relief. "Let's hope the impulsive wench **does** go directly to work," he thought.

Just then, he heard a rapid knock on the door. "In!" he called out.

The door opened, and Clovis Hobbs entered. "No luck."

"She's not at work," said Kelly. "I told the clerk to have her ring us directly she gets there."

"Then why the gloomy face? We've done all we could. And at least Ferguson is on to something."

"Yes," Kelly scowled. "But he's out there, whilst we're here, waiting-for an hysterical woman."

Kelly's scowl deepened. "But what if she makes fools of us?" he thought. "What if she goes straightaway to Paddington, and thence to Bodmin? She's high-strung and cunning enough to try it-you mark my words," he said.

"No need to worry on that score," Hobbs assured him.

"Why not?" asked Kelly.

"I rang the station-master at Paddington," Hobbs matter-of-fact replied. "His chaps will keep an eye open for us. I also rang Sgt. Andrews of the Paddington police station. He'll send a constable to the railway station to act on our behalf."

Hobbs was rightly pleased with his display of imagination and initiative.

"Head her off at the pass, eh? My compliments," said Kelly.

A moment later, the phone rang. Kelly answered it. "Inspector Kelly..."

"Janet Miller. I was told to ring you immediately. Has something happened?

"Yes. I'd like you to return here at once. We have some news for you."

"News? What news?"

"Too much, and too sensitive, to trust to a phone-call," was all that Kelly would say.

The woman thought quickly and anxiously. "And if I go to Bodmin on my own? What then?" she asked.

"The danger is too great," Kelly replied, as he recalled Ferguson's message. "Miss Miller, if you want our help, you must do as I tell you," he added, most emphatically. "The danger is too great, otherwise."

"Really?" she asked, defensive and challenging. "How great?"

"Your life. Is that great enough?"

CHAPTER 42

▼

A TANGLED SKEIN

A few minutes before five, there was knock on the door of Insp. Hobbs' office. Kelly and Hobbs were surprised when Janet Miller crossed the threshold. Her mood was more restrained than it had been that morning, though her concern and worry had not diminished.

She found John Kelly was far more comforting than he had been at their first meeting. He offered her a cup of warm herbal tea. Chilled and apprehensive, she looked at him, and then at Hobbs.

"One of our colleagues is in Bodmin now," Kelly told her. "With Sgt. Bailey. They were investigating another case when a lead took him to the Woodsons."

"I knew it!" Janet Miller exclaimed.

Kelly cocked his head sharply. "Knew what?" he wondered. Suddenly flustered, she said, "Why...why, that some thing is terribly wrong with Gwen. Jim Woodson is a hard, uncaring man. I wouldn't be surprised if the police suspect him of some wrongdoing. He turned Gwen against me—I'm certain he did."

Kelly glanced at Hobbs, and wondered just how much he should reveal to Janet Miller. Then, "We called you back here to warn you-to give you some idea-of the very serious nature of our case...of our grave concern..."

John Kelly was unusually concise. The young woman listened in stunned and incredulous silence, as he told his tale. When he finished, she pressed a trembling hand to her breast.

"Insp. Kelly and I are going to Bodmin, first thing tomorrow morning," Hobbs added. "Whatever mortal man can do to unravel this tangled skein, we shall do," he assured her.

"'Mortal man'?" she repeated. "I like that. What about 'mortal woman'?!" she insisted, despite her fatigue.

Kelly let Hobbs handle it.

"No-it's out of the question! The danger is too great."

Miss Miller was adamant. "My friend is in danger. I must help her!"

John Kelly rose and walked towards the young woman. She looked up, a trifle nervous, at the implacable expression on his lean face.

The detective put a hand on the back of her chair and leaned down. "Do you want to help? Very well. You will go home and you will lock your door and stay there until I say that you can leave. Do we understand each other?"

Janet Miller was surprised by Kelly's unexpected demand, yet part of her understood that it was for her safety.

Then, "As you wish, Inspector Kelly."

She rose, gloves in one hand, and handbag hanging from her shoulder. "You will keep me informed?"

She locked eyes with Kelly, then with Hobbs. Both men nodded.

A moment later, she was gone.

CHAPTER 43

▼

THE MITHRAEUM

Late Tuesday afternoon, Eliezer Jordan stepped off the train in Hexham. He checked into a room at a local inn. Tossing his bags onto the bed, he showered, changed his clothes, then went downstairs to order a meal from the kitchen.

Despite his hunger, he barely touched his food. Despite his fatigue, part of his mind continued to analyze the deadly, perplexing problem that had brought him to England.

It was to no avail. Try as he might, he could see no pattern-find no answers.

A brief walk after dinner provided some exercise, but no solutions to his puzzle. He returned an hour later, and went directly to bed.

The next morning, after a light breakfast, he rented a car and drove off.

A sense of some trepidation came over him as he neared his goal. What had he gotten himself into? What cruel enemy were he and his friends pursuing? he wondered, as he drove on.

He soon arrived at the ruins of a temple of the Persian sun god Mithra, by Hadrian's Wall, one of Britain's most famous antiquities. Parking the car, he got out, then leaned against the vehicle. He stood there, silently, his arms folded across his chest.

He stared at the ancient ruin. He wanted to get the feel of the place, and its role in this mystery. Then, he drew a deep breath, and approached this long-abandoned temple of an ancient Persian mystery cult.

He shuddered, but it was not from the cold. "Hmph! Have I become a little child, having nightmares even during the day? What can Celtic fairy-tales, and a Mithraic temple, do to me?"

A smile now came to his face. Then, he crossed the threshold, and entered the once-sacred confines. He walked around the time-worn area. His eyes took in everything as he made mental notes of his surroundings.

The centuries receded before him. In his mind's eye he saw Rome's legions honoring this martial deity. He pictured the youthful Mithra slaying an ox, and watching over his faithful followers.

Jordan was pleasantly surprised to see that the temple had been restored to an accurate semblance of its original state. How odd, he thought, that he, a Jew, should be standing in a temple built by Romans to the Persian god of fertility and sunlight, here in the realm of Druids, Celts, and Britons. "Quite a curious combination," he thought, with a warm, wry smile.

He now stood in the Mithraeum, the underground chapel in which the god's sacred, secret mysteries were once held. He imagined Imperial legions from the nearby fort of Brocolitia being initiated into the cult of Mithra, partaking of ceremonies involving real or symbolic tests of endurance—ceremonies which would enable them to enter the realms of light, over which Mithra himself was believed to preside.

He saw the celebrants being anointed with honey, then baptized, and sharing their holy meal of bread, water, and sacred wine. Thus would they be reborn, and become one with Mithra—Mithra, guardian of law, mediator between man and Ahura Mazda, watching over the faithful until his second coming. Mithra, whose religion abounded in astral symbolism, and who held out to his initiates the hope of salvation and resurrection.

The signs of the zodiac formed a basic part of the temple's decor. There was an ancient model of Mithra killing Geusha Urvan, the primeval ox, from whose body sprang all plants and animals beneficial to mankind.

Jordan lost track of all time as he stood there, scrutinized, and wondered. How full of secrets was this ancient place? What stories might its ghosts tell if they could return and speak?

He remained there for more than an hour. The mystic opened himself to the silence and solitude, absorbing some of the dormant vibrations while leaving some of himself behind, in exchange.

At last he emerged from the temple. He was glad to see the sun again, and feel the crisp, clean air on his face. Then, mindful of the task that had brought him here, Jordan put aside his scholarly interests and viewed the site from a different, far more serious perspective.

"Two bodies, methodically desecrated, were found here on October 28. Two murders," Jordan vocalized. "In a temple of Mithra.

"Mithra, the rock-born. Holder of the highest place in heaven, after Ahura Mazda. Tireless foe of sterility, suffering, and vice. Watching over the faithful until the day of his second coming. Whose adherents were sworn to chastity, to be reborn, spiritually, as the last part of their sacred ritual. Mithra, with his creed of redemption, grace, and eternal life. Mithra, born at the winter solstice, and reborn at the spring equinox."

The archaeologist's soft voice and measured tone served to relax him, and induce a trance-like state. Now, it was no longer Eliezer Jordan who stood there, silent and brooding, before this sanctuary of long-forgotten esoteric rites. It was Barad, the student of riddles. Barad, the enigma.

A great surge of energy began to flow through and around him.

His mind reached across the abyss of time. It came to rest in this same place millenia earlier. He beheld the temple as it was meant to be seen, being used as it was meant to be.

The vision sharpened at random intervals, revealing motion, color, a sense of purpose—then, it stopped abruptly.

Once more, Eliezer Jordan felt the cold air's invigorating kiss on his face. Was it a vision? Or simply a daydream?

He walked slowly, then came to a sudden halt as the first faint light of understanding came to him.

He signed. Then, he turned, crossed the parking lot, and stood by his car. He took a long last look at the rolling countryside then got into the car and returned to Hexham.

CHAPTER 44

▼

DANCING ANTLERS

Clovis Hobbs was worried. He had been waiting at Padding-ton since 8:20 AM. Two hours later, there was still no sign of John Kelly. Kelly was reliable and punctual to a fault; for him to be late for an appointment was most unique and newsworthy.

Hobbs rang Kelly's home twice, and the office three times—to no avail. A call to the Scotland Yard reception desk revealed that John Kelly had entered the building some time ago but had not been seen since.

Annoyed, he checked his watch. He was about to call the Yard yet again when he saw Insp. Kelly enter the giant structure. The man was in a foul mood, snapping at Hobbs almost immediately.

"Have you the tickets?"

Hobbs displayed them.

"Hang it all, Kelly, where have you been?" he asked, showing that he could be equally ill-tempered, as Kelly took his elbow and they rushed to the platform.

"I've been with bloody Oswald!" Kelly fumed. "Now, let's get on that blasted train."

Once on the train, Hobbs sat across from Kelly, who was in a black mood. After a time, the latter finally calmed down.

"Oswald wants to take Ferguson and me off the case. Oh, he's looking for you, too, since you invited yourself in."

"Me? But I distinctly recall—"

Kelly laughed, but it was a humorless laugh. "Relax, Hobbs. I was joking about you, but Oswald's serious about the rest of it."

"I suppose he's within his official rights," Hobbs sug-gested. "After all, he's duty-bound to use every means at his disposal to get the job done. If one thing doesn't work, you try something else, until you succeed, or give up."

"I'm aware of that," Kelly growled. "But Ferguson and I have cracked tough nuts before. We're good at what we do."

"What do you intend to do now?"

"Do? Now?" thought Kelly, almost absent-mindedly.

"Obviously—we're going to solve this damned bugger of a case. Let him bring us up on charges **then**."

"As bad as that, is it? You're taking a great profes-sional risk, Mr. Kelly. After all, Oswald is our commanding officer."

John Kelly said nothing.

"What will Ferguson say about this?" Hobbs then asked.

"He'll fume and fuss, I suspect. Then, he'll declare that we intend to solve the case, then toss a fait accompli into the lap of any hearing Oswald wants to convene."

With those words, Kelly removed his shoes, and planted his feet upon the opposite seat. Leaning back, he made himself comfortable. He closed his eyes, intending to sleep for the rest of their journey.

The afternoon was still young when they arrived at Bodmin.

The sky was crystal clear and the air most refreshing.

Hobbs and Kelly went to the police station, and entered with an eager step.

"Good afternoon, Constable," Kelly addressed the young woman at the front desk. "I'm Insp. Kelly of the Metropolitan Police. This is Insp. Hobbs. We'd like to see Sgt. Bailey, please."

"Oh, yes. Of course," she said. "Sgt. Bailey expected you here two hours ago. He and Insp. Ferguson have been out since lunch. They left word that you were to wait for them once you got here."

She escorted them to Bailey's office, and motioned them to a pair of comfortable seats. A moment later, she brought in some warm drinks—tea for Kelly, and cocoa for Hobbs.

It wasn't long before Ferguson and Bailey returned. The Scot greeted his two colleagues, and Bailey was introduced to Hobbs.

As they sat around Bailey's desk, Ferguson's face beamed with enthusiasm.

Kelly grinned. "You seem to be brimming with good news," he said. "Hobbs and I are most eager to hear it."

Ferguson and Bailey gave a thorough account of the events of the past few days. Kelly and Hobbs listened with keen interest. At the end of the narrative, Hobbs expressed his disbelief quite earnestly.

"Wailing banshees? Evil eyes? Horned gods of the nether world?" he said. "Good Lord!"

Bailey nodded towards Hobbs. "I agree with you, sir. It all sounds like mumbo-jumbo, but there are some very odd things going on."

"Can you fathom any of it?" Hobbs asked.

"Only tentatively, just now," said Bailey. "Three of the victims showed an active interest in ancient Celtic lore and customs. One of them actually left Rev. Thomson's church six years ago, and joined a druidic circle. That's our common thread so far—Celtic lore."

"Three? But there have been thirteen murders," Kelly recalled. "What of the other ten."

"After we found this initial link, we rang the police departments investigating those other deaths. They're checking the backgrounds of the other victims for similar interests."

"And now, it's your turn to tell us a few things," said Ferguson. "Tell me of your meeting with Miss Miller. And what you were able to learn about—what was it? Yes—the 'Festival of the Deer Men.'"

Hobbs spoke first. In a few brief minutes, he told of their meeting with the young woman, the previous day.

Now, they looked at Kelly with inquiring glances. The man produced a note pad from the inner pocket of his jacket. He cleared his voice and began.

"Let me see. Well, Ferguson, in answer to your curious request, I found four interesting tidbits. One book actually penned with an article on the 'Abbotts Bromley Horn Dance.' It's held on the Monday after the Sunday after 4 September, and is supposedly to be related to the deer-hunt—a form of ritual magic. There's also a brief description of the dance.

"A short entry in another book refers to the 'Abbotts Bromley Antler, or Horn, Dance.' The dance is described, and an ancient ritual significance attributed to it; it is said to be one of the few surviving animal dances in Europe.

"A brief reference in a third book implies a hold-over from prehistoric ritual magic. Finally, the author of another work ventured to suggest that the festival stems from the worship of Cernunnos, the powerful antlered dweller of the nether world—and, by the way, the prototype of the horned Christian Satan. The author also notes that on 13 September, the people of the Breton town of Carnac celebrate the 'pardon' of St. Cornely, the patron saint of horned animals."

The four men sat back and silently reflected upon their findings. For Ferguson and Kelly, there was the added thought that, with Jordan's timely help, they had made more progress these past few days than they had in four months.

The Scot's feeling of relief and satisfaction was, therefore, quite under-standable. In spite of it, a peevish expression now came to his friend's face.

"What is it?" asked Ferguson.

Kelly now told him of his summons to Oswald's office that morning, and of the unwelcome news he had received. Bailey looked at him in sur-prise and disbelief. Ferguson snorted in contempt.

"This is unexpected," said Bailey. "And most peculiar. Why should he want you off the case?"

He shook his head. "After all the work we've done. It's a bloody shame. What should we do now?"

"Do? Why, we'll solve this damned thing," replied Fergu-son, with some force. "Then, we'll toss a fait accompli onto the lap of any hearing Oswald wants to convene."

Kelly looked at Hobbs, smiled, and nodded.

CHAPTER 45

▼

A WORRIED POTTER

Janet Miller awoke Tuesday morning, after a fitful night's sleep. After her strange experience in Maidenwell, and her visits to the police, she was at a loss as to what to do next. Of this she was certain—that she would not sit idly by, in her cozy flat, while her friend was in danger.

Miss Miller had a quick breakfast. Then, she brushed her teeth and hair, packed a small bag, and went by underground to Paddington. Despite the warnings of Hobbs and Kelly, she would run the gauntlet of danger on her own.

Many miles to the west, in a cottage in St. Ives, Lle-wellyn Cardigan sat by his potter's wheel, but found that he could not work. He stood up, and walked restlessly around.

His wife heard him moving about. She came to the door of his workshop.

"What is it, Lyn?" she asked. "You've been moping since you got home from Redruth."

"Yes, I suppose I have been. But I've just spent a most peculiar week," he said, as he stopped his work, and told her of his experiences of the past few days.

"Odd, indeed," she agreed. "And certainly not what you expected when you went to London five days ago. All the same, I don't see why you're fretting so."

The man shook his head. "You may be right, dear. But ever since I came home, I've had this feeling—a sense of impending danger."

"Danger? What kind? For whom?" she wondered.

"For those two nice fellows at the Yard. And their Amer-ican friend. I don't know what the danger is, or when and where it will come, but the feeling is there, and quite annoying. I can't seem to shake it off."

His wife kissed him gently on the cheek. "In that case, why don't you ring them, and tell them what's on your mind? They seemed like such fine men; I'm sure they'll understand."

"Hmm—maybe," he quietly muttered.

Following her advice, he rang Scotland Yard, and asked to speak with John Kelly or Sean Ferguson.

"I'm sorry, sir, they're both out at the moment," a bus-inesslike voice told him. "Would you care to speak with some-one else?"

"No, thank you. If you should hear from either of them, please ask them to ring Cardigan, St. Ives. Yes, they have my number. It may be important. Thank you."

With that, he put the phone down. He was not the sort to worry need-lessly, yet one thought still bothered him. Why should he have this sense of impending danger? Or believe that something threatened the three men he had recently met in London?

Cardigan did not return to his potter's wheel. "What I need is a long, quiet walk," he decided. "And a good think. Have to find the cause of this nagging premonition."

So saying, he put on his coat, cap, and scarf, and stepped out into the cold, invigorating air. He walked, and thought, but found no answer. But he would have been relieved to know that one of the men he was thinking of would soon cross his threshold.

CHAPTER 46

▼

POOR, DEAR GWEN

Anxious yet resolute, Janet Miller arrived in Bodmin shortly after noon. She had an air of fear and tension as she hastened to a hotel. Fear and tension—quite understandable, given her nature and the circumstances.

"I must get to the bottom of this," she told herself, with a stubborn insistence, as she nervously unpacked her compact suitcase.

A warm, refreshing shower, followed by a nourishing meal, helped somewhat to soothe her taut nerves. And they gave her something else—something equally important. She now had time to sit perfectly still, and try to review this past hectic week, clearly and carefully.

"Why should Gwen wish to end our friendship?" she asked herself, for the twentieth time, as she sat in the privacy of her hotel room. "What has happened to her, these past three years? Why the frightening change in her appearance?" she wondered, as she sipped a mug of warm chocolate.

That she might be wrong never occurred to her. Nor did the idea that she should leave well enough alone—that some things were best left undisturbed, and unknown.

"I'm sure that Sgt. Bailey didn't believe me. He seemed to treat me like a frightened child," she recalled, with some displeasure. "He either can't—or won't—do anything. That much is obvious," she concluded.

"Those two men in London believe me now—I'm sure of that," she thought, with a smile. The idea gave her some comfort and assurance. "That Insp. Hobbs is a dear."

Now, the smile left her tired face, as if wiped away by an unseen hand. "Poor Gwen. Her husband may have deceived the police, but he hasn't misled me," she firmly decided. "He must have coerced her into standing by him."

In her anxiety, and naive concern, she never imagined that Gwen Woodson was in no danger—that she had willingly sought to dissolve their friendship; and freely sided with her husband when he lied to Sgt. Bailey.

Shortly after three o'clock, she left the hotel, and went in search of a taxi. In her present state of mind, she didn't notice a man who had gotten out of his car a few minutes earlier, and was now walking in her direction.

The man, however, took a quick passing note of her. Jim Woodson paused, and watched the young woman.

"Damnation! It can't be!" he tried to convince himself.

"That bitch doesn't give up, does she?"

Woodson hurried to the nearest public telephone. He thrust his hands into his coat pockets and took out some loose change. Depositing some coins, he quickly dialed a number.

"Damn it, Gwen, pick up the phone!" he cursed.

Finally, after four rings the phone was answered. "Yes? Gwen Woodson here."

"It's Jim. I'm glad I got you in time," he said, quickly.

Despite his outward composure, his mood clearly colored his voice. His wife noticed his worried tone. "Is something wrong?" she asked.

"I hope not. And I want to keep it that way."

"Why? What is it?"

"It's that girl again—that 'friend' of yours," he replied, coming to the point.

"It can't be. Are you sure?"

"Yes. I saw her not three minutes ago."

Gwen almost laughed under her breath. "She's persistent—I'll say that much for her."

"I'm sure that she'll head for the house, and try to speak with you."

Gwen's face wore a serious look, as her mind worked quickly. "Don't worry, Jim. I'll think of something," she assured him. Gwen Woodson could be cold, practical, and ruthless, when the occasion required. Her instincts told her that such an occasion was now approaching.

"Don't do anything hasty or rash, Jim. You take care of your errand. I'll handle her."

The man then put the girl out of his thoughts—there would be sufficient time to worry about her and any danger she posed, soon enough. Now, he would take care of the business that had brought him to Bodmin.

Less than a mile away, Janet Miller found a taxi. Her sense of anticipation increased as she got in, and told the driver, "Maidenwell, please," in a low, nervous voice.

A short ride brought her to the rustic hamlet. The car came to a halt. She hesitated before opening the door, as she recalled her reception there a few days earlier.

Miss Miller steeled herself, emerged from the cab, and walked towards the cottage with some trepidation. She stopped near the threshold and looked around.

With a slow, deliberate step, she walked up to the door, and knocked. There was no reply. She waited a moment, then knocked again.

It seemed an eternity before a pair of feet echoed within. Grasping the latch, Gwen Woodson pulled the door open a few inches.

"What are you doing here?" she asked, in a voice as frosty as the winter air.

More than just the threshold of the cottage stood between the two women as they looked at each other. "It is rather chilly out here, Gwen. May I come in?"

Without a word, Gwen stepped aside, then shut the door after Janet entered. She gestured toward the living room.

"Give me your coat, Jan. Would you care for a cup of tea?" she asked, rather noncommittally.

"No thank you—I just ate."

"You're looking well," said Gwen, after a brief, awkward silence. "How long has it been? Three—no, four years, isn't it?"

"Yes, four."

Gwen smiled a faint smile. "Four years," she said, as if thinking aloud. "It doesn't seem so. You've hardly changed—do you still go mountain-climbing?"

"Yes, I do. But there aren't any mountains here in Britain—only a few modest hills." She coughed a nervous cough.

"You've changed since I saw you last, Gwen. What happened?"

"People change," Gwen replied, as she sat up, and rested her hands on her lap. "Jim and I have found a new set of interests, since we've been married. And a new set of friends—people who are not of the world we knew as young girls."

There was something mystical and eerie about her as she spoke. She lit a cigarette, and sat there, pensive and aloof.

Janet narrowed her eyes. Gwen's manner was irritating—frightening—and Janet was now convinced that Jim Woodson had had some strange hold over his wife.

"Come back to London with me, Gwen," she insisted. "Leave this place. Leave that horrid man! I have friends who can help you."

"I do not wish to leave my husband," Gwen assured her.

"And I do not need any help. Go back home, Janet. Our paths once crossed, but now they've diverged. Never shall we trod the same path again."

So saying, she went to the coat-rack, and gave Janet her coat. "You'd best leave," she suggested, in a tone that could not be mistaken. "Do not trouble us again."

Janet didn't know what to say or do. She just sat there, silent and still. She had come there to satisfy her curios-ity, but Gwen had only increased her puzzlement, and the air of mystery. She had hoped to salvage their friendship, but now saw that that was impossible.

She stood and walked to the fireplace. Suddenly, she felt very cold and lonely. Neither the crisp, crackling fire nor the warm, tasty tea could dispel the chill that came over her.

At that moment, both women were startled by a sudden noise. They turned. The front door opened and Jim Woodson entered. A blast of cold Cornish air accompanied the grim-faced man.

Surprise and annoyance were clearly written on his face, when he saw Janet. "Still here? Some people don't know when they aren't welcome."

Janet looked at him with a haughty sneer. "Poor Gwen," she said, in a tone of undisguised pity and contempt. "What a delightful bastard you've married. Well, perhaps you deserve each other."

She said no more. She snatched her coat from Gwen, put in on, and hurried outside. There had been no time to call a cab, but given her experiences with the Woodsons, a long walk now seemed most welcome.

With an expression of scorn on her pretty face, she turned her back on the Woodsons. As conflicting emotions raced through her mind, she made her way back to Bodmin.

CHAPTER 47

▼

GOING TO ST. IVES

Eliezer Jordan awoke quite early, that cold Thursday morning. He had now been in England for one week.

"What a week it's been," he reflected, silently, as he sat at a table, eating breakfast. Pensively, he gazed out the window. The sky was a dirty gray, and swirling flurries of snow were dancing mischievously down from the heavens.

Returning briefly to his room, he packed his tote bag. Going downstairs, he paid his bill. A short walk brought him to the railway station.

Bundled up against the cold, he stood and waited. His eyes traveled from side to side, studying and enjoying the scene that stretched silently before him. With his inner eye, he thought of the case that had brought him here—of all that he had learned, and done—and of the task that still confronted him.

His thoughts, and his solitude, were soon interrupted. A mechanical melody that rarely failed to enchant him signaled the arrival of his train. He found a seat in one of the coaches, sat back, and made himself comfortable.

As the train rolled onward, his eyes watched the landscape speed by. Retreating within, he thought of Ferguson and John Kelly, and of the problem that had brought him to England. Had his friends made any progress, these past few days?

He thought of the many pieces of the puzzle that he now held.

· Mentally, he arranged and rearranged them, to form a variety of curious patterns. It was fairly easy for him to sense some dark, sinister power. Who was wielding it? And for what deadly purpose?

Alas, Jordan didn't know—though he was most eager to know.

As he traveled south and west, he found himself thinking of something else—of a priceless book of ancient Welsh tales that he had unexpectedly been given. He thought, too, of Llewellyn Cardigan, the man who had given him the gift. He smiled warmly as he recalled their meeting. Then, his smile became a frown of puzzlement as he relived their visit to the museum, and that peculiar 'lecture' they had gone to.

Almost instinctively, his hand reached into the pocket of his shirt. He took out a small brown envelope, opened it, and removed a small, round object.

"Hmm—I've been meaning to ask about this," he reminded himself. "That gives me an idea," he thought, as his whole being now lit up with a warm, animated light.

"I won't go back to Bodmin—not just now, at least," he decided. "I think a slight detour is advisable. I'd like to pay a call on Mr. Cardigan. I sense that it might be very rewarding."

So it was that Jordan chose to go to St. Ives, rather than to Bodmin.

Arriving in Manchester, he made the first of several changes of trains. He also made a brief phone-call.

"Mr. Cardigan? Eliezer Jordan. I'm glad I got you in. No—Manchester. Will you be home this evening? I need some help with a jigsaw puzzle. It might interest you. I'll explain everything then. Dinner? Of course. Thank you. Good-bye."

That evening, Jordan was in St. Ives. He wanted only two things just now—to wash, then rest for an hour or so.

He went directly to the Cardigan home. He was grateful for the warm welcome he received, and for the fact that here was someone who might be able to help him. And the smells from the kitchen were quite tantalizing.

At last, he and his hosts were seated at a table, with cups of warm cocoa. The atmosphere might have been as warm, but there were signs of worry in the air.

Jordan studied the Cardigans carefully, then, "Something is obviously on your minds—do you want to tell me about it?"

Cardigan exchanged glances with his guest.

"Your arrival is providential," he said. "I know that you've studied the mysteries of the past, but I sense that you also study the true mysteries—those forces which have no physical substance."

Jordan nodded. "I do. But one doesn't need mystical powers to see that you're highly concerned about something. What is it?"

Husband and wife exchanged glances. They felt the need to confide in someone—to relieve themselves of a weighty burden. In their present frame of mind, they saw Jordan's arrival as providential, and viewed him as one who naturally inspired trust.

"Do you recall out meeting in London, last Thursday?" Cardigan began, a bit nervously. Jordan did, though it now felt as more than one week had gone by, since then.

"After you and I parted company, I spent the evening with Mr. Kelly. An interesting fellow, and very sensitive," he observed.

"Friday morning, I went by train to Redruth, where I was to attend a meeting Sunday afternoon," he went on. "The week-end passed uneventfully—until very late Sunday night, that is."

"What happened?" Jordan asked.

"We were awakened by the sound of our dog howling," Edith Cardigan relied. "It wasn't an ordinary cry—she seemed positively terrified."

A life-long animal-lover, Jordan knew that the instincts of animals were very sensitive, and quite reliable. "I sup-pose you came downstairs, to see what was she was reacting to. What did you find?"

They hesitated. The memory was still very fresh, and very upsetting.

"Yes, we did," the man replied. "We opened the door, and found some-thing bizarre—obscene."

"What was it?"

"It was a straw basket containing a sheep's heart, surrounded by a ring of pine cones."

Two images immediately came to Jordan's mind—the dream that he had recently dreamt, and the scene in the Bodmin church.

"Did you notify the police?" he asked.

"Yes," the woman told him. "But they viewed it as a crude 'practical joke,'" she said.

"Did anything happen after that?"

"Three days later, our terrier was murdered. We found her, hanging from a tree, by her hind legs," the bitter man replied.

A sad, heavy silence filled the bright, tidy room. It was easy for Jordan to sympathize with them.

"We went back to the police," Edith Cardigan added. "This time, they were more inclined to listen. They promised to look into it."

Jordan rubbed his mouth pensively. "Can you think of any-one who might want to do this? Someone whom you might have angered, perhaps?"

"Not that we know of," said the woman, after some thought.

"And the strange thing is, that when we mentioned it to two friends, both had had similar experiences—one Monday, and one yesterday."

"Gruesome," Jordan thought, with a grimace. Then, "Do you remem-ber our visit to the British Museum?" he asked his host, after a thoughtful silence. "And your refutation of that—what did he call himself? Yes— 'keeper of the ley lines.'"

"Yes—Andrew Barrett," Cardigan recalled, with a frown. "I met him and his 'druid', Malcolm Morgan, twice before. We crossed paths—and verbal swords—again, at that meeting this past Sunday."

"Hmm. He was quite put out when you dared challenge his beliefs. I'm sure that he must have some animosity," Jordan suggested. "Of course, I'm not accusing him of anything—only making a suggestion."

"Would he really resort to something so vengeful and vicious?" Edith asked.

"It depends on his character, and how provoked he felt. I noted his reaction to your husband's challenge. I could easily suspect him of harboring hostile feelings towards you."

"Yes, it is a possibility," Cardigan agreed, after a brief silence. "But it's only a suspicion, not actual proof."

Llewllyn Cardigan shook his head ruefully, then changed subjects. "It's in the hands of the police now, Professor, so why don't you tell us what brings you to our doorstep?"

Jordan took a deep breath, and let it out with a huff. He had no wish to add to their problems or worries, but didn't know what else to do.

As concisely as he could, he told them why he had come to England, and what he had experienced in that very busy week.

"The police must truly be frustrated, to ask an outsider for help," said Cardigan. "Especially someone who isn't like a criminal investigator by profession."

"They certainly are," Jordan agreed, with a smile. "But officially, Scotland Yard hasn't called me in on the case. Ferguson called me, and asked for my help as a personal favor. As far as the Metropolitan Police are concerned—as far as I am concerned—Ferguson and Kelly are still in charge of the investigation. And they'll get full credit if and when this case is finally solved."

"'If,'" Cardigan echoed. "The biggest word in the English language."

"It certainly is, isn't it?" said Jordan.

"Our problems share two things, at least," Mrs. Cardigan then noted. "A wicker basket was left in the Bodmin church last Saturday, and a straw one on our doorstep, on Monday. And each of the victims, human and animal, was mutilated in some way. How awful," she said, in a heavy whisper.

"Balor—Cernunnos—Banshees? Most odd," her husband said. "Odd, and ominous. Whoever is behind all this knows what he is doing, and why. Be on your guard, Professor—at all times. You and your two friends are up against a reso-lute enemy."

"Thanks for the warning—and for your concern," said Jordan. "I know that—just as I know that his anonymity adds to the danger. We don't know who he is, or when or where he'll strike, next."

"Have you any suspicion as to who that enemy might be?" asked Cardigan.

"Right now—not the slightest, I'm afraid," Jordan admitted.

He shrugged his shoulders. Then, recalling something, he reached into his shirt pocket, and removed a small, round object. "Do you know what this is?" he asked his hosts.

By way of reply, Cardigan took a book off the shelf, and began to thumb through it.

"Ah, yes," he finally said. "Here we are. Here's a photo of some pieces recently uncovered in an ancient Celtic tomb. Archaeologists believe that they were used in a game similar to ludo, a game derived from parchisi. They're exactly like the one that you have."

Jordan looked, then shook his head. "Balor—Mithra–wailing banshees. Now—parchisi!" Despite the grotesque nature of the case, he could not repress a smile.

"If we can help in any way, please let us know," his kindly hosts assured him.

"Thanks. I will. And thanks for a delicious meal. But I think there's not much more that I can do today," he said, glancing at the clock.

"It's only six o'clock," said Cardigan. Why not join us in the sitting room for awhile. Edith and I would welcome the company—perhaps we can tell you something about the history of Cornwall, and of our ancient Celtic heritage."

Jordan welcomed the opportunity. For the next two hours, and again for most of the following day, Jordan received his first real introduction to the history of Cornwall, and of the ancient Celtic culture.

At last, he retired to the room that the Cardigan's had put at his disposal.

For two hours, he sat in solitude and silence, as he gave the Sabbath a private, belated welcome. Although he consi-dered himself a humanist, secularist, and skeptic, Jordan had a healthy respect for tradition, and for the moral and spir-itual value of the Sabbath

For two hours, he sat on the floor in deep, relaxing medi-tation. Then, the change took place. The mind of the scholar moved aside, and a mysti-cal entity glided to the fore. As it did, he heard a faint yet recognizable melody.

Then, two Hebrew letters flashed before his mind's eye. They lasted just long enough for him to see them, and to understand their meaning.

That night, he slept fitfully. A series of images flashed through his mind. They challenged him to decipher their cryptic message, and to use that message to solve a deadly mystery.

At last, his restlessness subsided. He listened carefully, and heard a joy-ous melody. Then, he heard two simple words—the first two words of the 95th. Psalm. That was all.

CHAPTER 48

▼

MAKING HEADWAY

Eliezer Jordan awoke early that Saturday morning. With an eager step, he hurried downstairs, to join his hosts for breakfast. He was brimming with anxious energy as he greeted them.

"You're very excited this morning," Cardigan observed, with a warm smile.

Jordan thought for a minute. "Yes—yes, I would say so. Tell me, Mr. Cardigan—did stone pillars have any special significance in ancient Celtic culture?"

"Why, yes," Cardigan replied. "In fact, the British land-scape is dotted with countless thousands of them, as you might already know. Some are solitary, and many are in—oh, I would say at least 2,000 henges and circles of various shapes and sizes."

Cardigan left the table momentarily. He returned with a handsome book of maps, photos, and text. "These maps show the distribution and locations of those circles and henges. And here is a diagram of the five principle shapes of those rings of stone."

Jordan studied the illustrations carefully.

"Have you found something?" Mrs. Cardigan asked him, after a polite silence.

"Yes, I think so. Last week, a straw basket was left by your door. And a wicker basket was left in the vicar's study, in Bodmin. Does that mean anything to you? Especially in the context of ancient Celtic beliefs or customs?"

Husband and wife exchanged puzzled glances. "I have a vague recollection of reading something about them," said the woman. "I think that Caesar wrote that the Gauls burned condemned criminals in huge wicker cages; their priests, the Druids, foretold the future by the movements of the dying bodies."

"Hmm. Interesting. Now, what about parts of the bodies? The head, for example. Had they any particular importance?"

"Yes, they did," Cardigan told him. "Quite often, Celtic warriors cut off the heads of their slain enemies. They kept them as trophies, and hung them on the posts of their huts, so that the spirits would protect them from misfortune."

Jordan's mind was working quickly. "Was this practice widespread?"

"Yes. In fact, the 'Cult of the Severed Head' was a major cult in the old religion."

"May I use your phone?" asked Jordan, with a sense of urgency.

"Of course."

He dialed a number in Bodmin, and waited anxiously while the phone rang. When it was answered, he identified himself, and asked for Sgt. Bailey.

The line clicked on hold, then, "Prof. Jordan! Good morn-ing. What can I do for you?"

"I think I've just solved part of our mystery. By the way, how is Rev. Thomson?"

"You haven't heard. He had an accident. Three days ago. Hit-and-run driver. Yes, he's alive, but in guarded condi-tion."

"Well, you'd better place a guard near him, Sergeant. I fear another attempt to kill him."

"Kill him?! Are you joking?! Who would want to do that?!"

"Our murderer—that's who. Now, is Ferguson there?"

The puzzled Sergeant quickly passed the phone to his colleague. "Yes? Professor? What's going on?" the Scot asked.

"I may have identified your murderer—with some help from two friends," Jordan told him. His tense body began to relax, and his face wore a satisfied smile. "I'll tell you everything when I see you. What about you? Have you and Kelly made any headway?"

"Yes, I think so. It's been a most interesting week. But where are you? When and where can we meet you?"

"I'm in St. Ives. I'll call you as soon as I've made my plans. And you'd better keep your eyes open—we're up against a ruthless adversary."

"You're telling me?" asked the Scot, with a shudder. "Now, what's this discovery you've made? Who do you think our killer is?"

"Not 'who,' but 'what,'" Jordan replied. "I suspect that someone has revived an ancient Celtic religious cult. Yes—the 'Cult of the Severed Head.'"

CHAPTER 49

▼

"WHEN DO WE LEAVE?"

"The Cult of the Severed Head?! Are you sure?" an in-credulous Llewellyn Cardigan asked. "How do you know?"

Eliezer Jordan simply nodded. It was the quiet, confident nod of one who knew precisely what he was saying. There was no doubt in his mind that he was correct.

The Cardigans looked at him in disbelief. "These murders were terrible enough, before," Edith remarked, in an obvious understatement. "If you're correct—if the Cult has been revived—it adds to the horror, and the tragedy."

"Assuming that you're correct, what will you do, now?" asked Cardigan, after his initial surprise subsided.

"I'd like to visit that fellow we met at the museum. Do you know any-thing about him?"

"His name is Andrew Barrett," Cardigan replied. "He and I crossed paths several times. He and his 'druid,' Malcolm Morgan, live in St. Buryan, a village near Penzance."

"Near Penzance? Hmm. How far is it from here? And how can I get there?"

"It's only five or six miles to Penzance, and another five or six to St. Buryan. We can drive directly there. When do we leave?" the Cornishman eagerly volunteered.

It was now Jordan's turn to be surprised.

"'We'?" he asked, then shook his head firmly. "No—it's out of the question. I appreciate the offer, but the risks are too great. You can do something far more helpful and important, if you don't mind."

"Of course. Whatever we can," the Cardigans agreed. "I'd like you to coordinate any messages between the police and myself. I gave Insp. Ferguson your phone number, and told him that I'm here. If he or Kelly should call, tell them where I've gone, and why. If I call you with any news, you can get it to them care of Sgt. Bailey of the Bodmin police."

"Yes—of course. But what if we don't here from you? What should we do?"

"Hmm—I'm so used to working alone, I hadn't thought of it. Let me see. Give me three days. If I haven't phoned by then, call Sgt. Bailey and tell them to bring the cavalry," he said, with a faint smile. "I guess that covers everything."

Slowly, almost reluctantly, he put on his warm down jacket and woolen scarf. With his hands thrust firmly in his pockets, and his shoulders hunched slightly forward, Eliezer Jordan left the warmth and coziness of the Cardigan cottage. Off he went, to play his part in a dangerous game.

CHAPTER 50

▼

PREMONITIONS

A dozen miles away, a winter-wrapped St. Buryan was already wide awake, and its people going busily about their daily affairs. As noon approached, Ellen Chatham was walking with a determined step to the home of Andrew Barrett. Under her left arm, she carried a cloth bag; in it were her ever-present needles and wool.

Barrett answered her knock, and let her in with an unan-swered welcome. She quickly made herself at home. Resting her bag on the floor, she removed its contents, and began to knit in silence.

"It's been arranged," she finally said. "The cycle will end as planned. We gather at Cairn Euny. Tuesday evening will see the final sacrifice."

"Well, that's something," said Barrett, with a sense of nervous relief. "Who will it be? Anyone we know?"

"No. The Woodsons selected her. A New Zealand girl—a former friend of Gwen's. Gwen had chosen to end their friendship, but the wench was persistent—refused to let well enough alone. She made two trips to Maidenwell—wanted to know why Gwen had ended their relationship."

"Nosy little tart, isn't she? She learned nothing, I hope," Barrett asked, with understandable concern.

"No. And she had no idea of what she's facing. It won't be the first time that curiosity has killed a cat," Ellen noted. All the while, she kept knitting—one would think that she was preparing for a quilting bee, not a ritual murder.

Barrett poured drinks for himself and the woman. "I hope that it goes as well as the others. The gods have been with us, so far. I should hate to see us press our luck."

Ellen's sharp green eyes looked at him. "This is unlike you, Andrew. You're not the sort to let fears or misgivings get the better of you."

"I know. Perhaps it's a premonition. Perhaps I'm still annoyed at Cardigan's effrontery at the Museum last week."

"Oh—that? You shouldn't be. It's bad for your composure," she gently chided him. "But it's odd, you're speaking of a premonition. Alice had one twice this week—including last night."

Ellen felt a moment of unease because she truly respected Alice Morgan's psychic abilities.

At that moment, an unexpected knock at the door interrupted them. The woman's hands ceased their constant motion.

The couple exchanged anxious glances. Barrett put his mug on the mantelpiece, and walked cautiously to the door. A strong hand reached out, and opened it.

"Andrew Barrett?" asked a firm, level voice.

"Yes. Who are you? What do you want?" he asked, defensively.

"My name is Jordan. I'm an American archaeologist. I'm doing some research—after hearing you speak in London last week, I decided to look you up, in the hope that you might help me."

There was a brief, awkward silence.

"May I come in and warm up for a minute?" the stranger asked.

"It's pretty chilly out here."

Reluctantly, Barrett stepped aside, and let him enter. There was an uneasiness in the room, as the three people looked at each other.

Ellen soon resumed her knitting, though she remained very much alert to the visitor's presence. Barrett poured some hot chocolate for Jordan then asked, "What would you like to know?"

"I'm doing some research on Eastern mystery cults in the Roman Empire. I'm curious to know if any of them reached Britain, and if they had any following among the local population."

"Mystery cults?" asked Ellen. "We know of none ever having reached Britain. Our own culture has always been sufficient for us. Our teachers, the druids, mastered the great cosmic truths long ago. There has never been any need among our people for any foreign creeds," she said, with an absolute certainty.

Jordan said nothing.

Barrett lifted his mug, and took another drink.

"I'm afraid that I must agree with Miss Chatham," he said, as he tried to hide his annoyance at this unforeseen intru-sion.

"Besides, I should think that you've chosen a rather difficult topic. There were many such cults. Are you interested in any specific one?"

"Yes. I'm looking into the cult of Mithra, the ancient Persian god of light. The Romans worshipped him, and may have brought that worship to Britain."

Barrett paced the room slowly. A feeling of uneasiness was simmering, just below the surface.

"Who the hell is he?" he wondered. "What does he want?"

He looked at the stranger. "I'm afraid I can tell you very little," he finally said. "Even if Mithra did reach our shores, I doubt that he had much of a local following. Our ancestors kept their cultural contacts with the Romans to a minimum," he assured Jordan.

He lit a cigarette. There was no mistaking his attitude—it was a clear invitation for Jordan to leave. Taking the hint, Jordan buttoned his coat, and walked towards the door. He took a few steps, then paused. He rubbed the side of his nose, and smiled.

"I almost forgot—there were two other things I wanted to ask."

"Yes? What are they?" asked Barrett, who made no effort to hide his annoyance. Ellen, the meanwhile, continued her knitting—with an added intensity, it seemed.

"Has either of you ever heard of Cernunnos? Or of the Cult of the Severed Head?"

CHAPTER 51

▼

PIECES OF A PUZZLE

It was early on a bright Monday afternoon. The four men came to Bodmin's police station, and entered Sgt. Bailey's office. Three of them went to their usual seats, while one paused, to study a large map on the wall. Then, he joined the others.

"Well, gentlemen," asked Ferguson. "What have we learned, since last we met? Anything useful and interesting?"

"We may have," said Kelly. "I'll let Hobbs tell you about it, since it was he who first noticed it."

"Very well, gentlemen," Hobbs began. "I owe this discovery to a life-long interest in antiquities, and to the fact that, as a boy, I wanted to be an antiquarian. Let me see," he thought, as he got up, walked to the wall, and checked several points on the map.

"Thanks to your friend, Ferguson, two very important facts have come to light—the element of Celtic mythology, and the fact that the sites of these dreadful murders form a tri-angle, with Bodmin, Brocolitia, and London as its corners."

He now tapped the map with some emphasis. "It was late Saturday evening that I noticed something else. With four exceptions, each murder was committed within a dozen miles of a prehistoric stone monument, or a site of some ancient sig-nificance. And even those exceptions are noteworthy."

"You don't say?" asked Bailey. "What might they be? And why mention them?"

"Well, to name but a few, Sergeant—Trethevy Quoit, and the 'Hurlers' stone circle, are about ten miles from here. The ancient site of Bratton Camp is within walking distance of Westbury. And over here," he pointed to a spot on the map, "is another stone circle on the A234, between Chipping-Norton and Long Compton."

"What of the exceptions?" Kelly asked.

"Well, to name but a few, Sergeant—Trethevy Quoit, and the 'Hurlers' stone circle, are about ten miles from here. The ancient site of Bratton Camp is within walking distance of Westbury. And over here," he pointed to a spot on the map, "is another stone circle on the A234, between Chipping-Norton and Long Compton."

"What of the exceptions?" Kelly asked.

"Glastonbury Tor—a site revered by 'ley liners' and others of that sort; Brocolitia, with its temple of Mithra; London Wall; and St. Paul's Cathedral."

"But the two sites in London—what makes them signifi-cant?" Kelly pressed him.

"Didn't you know? Well, London Wall is in Ludgate Hill," Mr. Hobbs replied. "Mark that name well, gentlemen, for it contains the name of Llud, an ancient Celtic deity surnamed 'the Cloudmaker.' He was also known as 'Nuada of the Silver Hand,' for he had lost an arm in battle, and was fitted with a silver prosthesis. As for the Cathedral," he solemnly concluded, "it stands on the site of a temple of this same ancient deity."

He drew a deep breath, and let it out with a huff. He was pleased with his discovery, and with the fact that he was able to share it with them.

"In view of what we've learned, I suspect two things," Hobbs good-naturedly volunteered, after Ferguson posed those questions. "The sites of these murders may have been chosen for their proximity to those ancient places. Indeed, the victims may have been killed at those prehistoric sites, then moved elsewhere, to mislead us."

"Let's assume that you're correct," Bailey suggested, after a brief silence. "Then, if other murders are to be committed, they're likely to be at or near some ancient monument. If so, where? And when?"

"The next murder will probably occur late one night this week," Kelly soberly predicted, with a calm air of certainty.

"Really? Why?"

"Last Sunday was the winter solstice—the day of the year with the fewest hours of light, and most of darkness. I once read that that day, and the week or two following, were once held in great awe and dread—Walpergisnacht and all that."

An apprehensive silence now filled the air. It was Sgt.

Bailey who finally broke it.

"If that's the case, gentlemen, we're in for a very busy week. I suggest a hearty supper. I don't know about you, but I'm famished. And we don't know what surprises Fate has in store for us."

CHAPTER 52

▼

THUNDER AND HAIL

"Has either of you ever heard of Cernunnos? Or of the Cult of the Severed Head?" the stranger wondered.

His question came as an unexpected and unpleasant surprise to his two reluctant hosts. Their discomfort was obvious, much as they tried to hide it.

Once again, Ellen's knitting came to a brief, perturbed halt. This time, however, there was a barely perceptible change in her forceful, self-assured manner. She and her tense companion exchanged worried glances. The man nodded his head ever so slightly; his eyes wore a hard look of caution, as he did.

"Cernunnos is the antlered god of the nether world," Ellen finally replied. "He of the deer's head is associated with a ram-headed serpent, and sometimes with 'Tavros Trigaranos'–'the bull with three cranes.' The bull was often depicted with three horns, and is a sacred synbol of strength and virility."

A look of rapture came to her cherubic face, as she fell into a thought-ful silence. Then, as her rapture subsided, another look came to her face. She was thinking that she may have said just a bit too much. After all, who was this stranger? What was his business here? What did he want with them?

Barrett lit a cigarette, as his annoyance and anxiety diminished a bit. Nonchalantly, he poured another round of drinks.

"There's very little to tell about—what was it? Yes—the 'Severed Head,' I'm afraid," he said, with a superficial smile.

"A few Greek and Roman historians here and there mentioned it—Diodorus, Tacitus, Caesar. But all were clearly biased against anything not Greek or Roman. Their writings contained too much misinformation, exaggeration, and misunderstanding to be of any real value."

"I see," said Jordan, casually. "So, you know very little about it, I gather."

"I see," said Jordan, casually. "So, you know very little about it, I gather."

The man nodded. "Only that it's been shrouded by the mists of time, and by centuries of legends, fear, and flights of fancy. Much like many other popular myths—UFO's, the Loch Ness monster, the Abominable Snowman."

"And ley lines, I should think," Jordan added.

The others tensed noticeably.

With a shrug of his shoulders, Jordan buttoned his coat and turned to leave. "Thanks for the help, all the same," he said. "If you should recall anything, or know anyone who can help me, I'm staying in Penzance, at the **Trelawny Arms.**"

He opened the door, and was about to leave, when the woman spoke.

"Perhaps you can tell us something."

He paused. "Yes? What is it?"

"What do you know about hailstones?" she asked, anxiously.

Jordan knitted his brow, then smiled a warm, confident smile.

"'So Moses stretched forth his hand towards heaven," he replied. "Then the Lord sent down thunder and hail, and fire ran down to the earth. And the Lord caused hail upon the land of Egypt, very grievous, such as had not been seen in all the land of Egypt since it became a nation."

CHAPTER 53

▼

GRIM AND RESOLUTE

Scarce had their caller gone when a grim, resolute Andrew Barrett got a coat and put it on.

"Come along, Ellen," he said in an urgent tone. "We've no time to lose."

Once again, her needles came to a halt. This had never happened before, and she was finding it most upsetting.

"What is it? Where are you off to?" she asked, as he tossed her needles and wool into her bag.

"To see Malcolm," was his terse reply, as they hastened out the door.

In a matter of minutes, they reached the Morgan home. Barrett knocked sharply on the door. A few seconds later, Alice Morgan opened it, and bade them enter.

"What's wrong, Andrew? You look positively on edge. Come in—give me your coats."

They removed their sturdy jackets. The man then walked to the fireplace, while Ellen found a comfortable chair. Immediately, she removed her needles and wool from her bag, and resumed her endless knitting.

"Andrew's not here just now—there's a problem at the mine—but I expect him soon. What is it? Ellen, won't one of you please tell me what's going on?"

"We've just had an unexpected visitor, Andrew and I," Ellen finally replied. She made no effort to disguise her inner feelings, as her nervousness churned up through her pudgy, self-assured exterior.

Barrett scowled, and flung a half-smoked cigarette into the fireplace.

"A visitor? Who? What did he want? By the Cauldron! I've never seen either of you looking so despondent," Alice observed, with a jesting smile.

"Hmph!" Ellen snorted, without missing a stitch. "Laugh if you must. It wasn't you who had the visitor."

"Very well, Ellen. You had a visitor. What of it? You still haven't told me who he was, or why his visit got you so upset."

"Upset? Why? What's happened?" a new voice asked. It was Malcolm Morgan. He took off his coat, poured a mug of warm chocolate, and flavored it with something stronger. "Why are you two so upset?" he asked his friends.

"A fellow named Jordan called on me, a short while ago," said Barrett. "He asked a few questions—uncomfortable questions. About Mithra, and Cernunnos. And about the Cult," he added, ominously.

Instinctively, Morgan tightened his grip on his mug. A hard expression came to his rough-hewn face, and his sharp, deep-set eyes glowed angrily.

"Jordan—Jordan," he muttered, knitting his furrowed brow.

"Damn! Why should that name sound so familiar?"

"Do you recall my visit here, last week ago?" Barrett reminded him. "It was the night the vicar was here. You said something about someone named Jordan. Remember?"

A brief silence followed, as Morgan recalled the incident.

"Yes," he said, slowly. "Yes, Andrew, I do. I do remember the name—and the man. That Kabbalist who interfered at Tintagel two years ago. And who came here now, to work with Ferguson and Kelly."

He took another drink, as his mood became more animated.

"Well, Andrew," he said, after a moment's thoughtful silence, "I see now why you're upset. From what I've hear, this fellow is someone to be reckoned with."

With his hands thrust firmly in his pockets, the druid began to pace the floor in deep, anxious thought.

"Malcolm, what is it?" his wife pressed him.

He paused, and looked at her with a strange light in his eyes. He thought carefully before answering.

"I can't say, precisely," he finally replied, in a cautious tone. "But I have a feeling that we may soon encounter your 'hailstone.'"

Alice Morgan was unprepared for her husband's remark. It had been enough for her that she had had a dire premonition twice this past week. But now—to think that her vision had assumed solid form—that that form had come to her hamlet, and spoken to the two friends now in her sitting-room.

The two men became concerned when they saw her complexion lose its color. Even Ellen looked up from her knitting long enough to notice Alice's ghostly pallor. As the blood briefly left Alice's face, Andrew and Malcolm rushed to her side, and helped her to the sofa.

Two tense minutes passed before she recovered. She felt a cold face cloth being gently yet firmly applied to her face and forehead.

"Take care," she whispered, when she found her voice. "We must take care. This man has great knowledge—of a kind I can't fathom."

Soon, her normal composure returned. Slowly, she sat up, and exchanged anxious glances with the others.

"I suppose this calls for a policy of watchful waiting," her husband thought, aloud. With a confident air, he got up, and poured drinks for himself, his wife, and their two friends. He lit a cigarette, and held it firmly in his hand, as he bit his lower lip thoughtfully. Now, he rubbed his thumb back and forth across his chin, and smiled—a sinister, scheming smile that boded no good.

CHAPTER 54

▼

THE INVITATION

Sunday came and went, as did most of Monday. For two days, Eliezer Jordan strolled along the streets of Penzance in a vain effort to put his mind at rest. He had been feeling an increasing tension since his return from St. Buryan, and wanted to minimize or eliminate it, before it got the better of him.

He awoke early, Sunday morning, and tried to put all thoughts of the case aside. He was only partially successful. That day, and again on Monday, he was wondering what his next move should be. He thought of his two friends—had they made any progress, since he last saw them?

Early Monday evening, he was sitting at a table in the guesthouse, with a simple meal in front of him. Hungry though he was, he was in no real mood to eat. For almost an hour, he sat there, idly toying with his food.

Suddenly, he sensed something in the back of his mind. Shedding his lethargy, he became watchful and wary.

Scarce had this feeling come over him than he heard an unfamiliar voice mention his name. Automatically, he sat up.

"The time has come," something seemed to warn him.

An eager smile came to his face. He moved his plate to one side. Turning his head ever so slightly, he saw a tall, sharp-featured man walking towards him.

With his smooth, silent gait, and piercing, weather-beaten face, the newcomer had the bearing of a stealthy hunter. In fact, that was what he was—though he didn't know that his prey had actively sought this meeting, and was as adept at the chase as he.

"Mr. Jordan? May I join you?"

"That chair is empty. Suit yourself," was the simple reply.

The stranger sat down, and ordered a drink.

"Who are you?" asked Jordan. "What do you want?"

"My name is Morgan. Malcolm Morgan. You called on a friend of mine two days ago."

"Did I? I didn't know we had any mutual acquaintances."

"It was in St. Buryan. His name is Andrew Barrett," Morgan reminded him.

"Barrett? Oh, yes—the fellow at the museum."

"He and Miss Chatham are neighbors of mine. They told me of your visit, and your questions. You're eager to learn something of our culture, I understand."

Jordan shifted his position slightly. "Yes, I am. But they were unable to tell me anything, I'm afraid." Or unwilling, he thought to himself.

Morgan's manner became animated, like a hunter who had found his quarry, and was about to bait and trap it. "They told me what you were looking for, so I took the liberty of calling on you."

"Really? In that case, would you mind answering the questions that they couldn't?" asked Jordan, in a firm, level tone.

"Not at all," Morgan readily replied. "I'd be more than happy to satisfy your curiosity. In fact, you might even want to return with me to St. Buryan. My wife and I would be glad to share our heritage and hospitality with you," he politely insisted.

Instinctively, Jordan felt defensive.

"Who is he?" he wondered. "What's his game? Well, that's what I came here to learn."

He looked through the window and gazed briefly at the cold, clear, starry sky. Then, he looked at Morgan.

"It's pretty late, Mr. Morgan," he finally said. "I had hoped to call it a night. And I wouldn't want to impose in any way."

"It's no trouble at all," Morgan assured him. "We'd be most disappointed if you refused."

"'We'?"

"Yes. My wife and I, and some friends. We'd all be quite willing to help you in any way we can."

"Well, you might be right," Jordan finally agreed. "Let me go to my room, and get my things."

Without waiting for a reply, he got up and went to his room. He returned shortly, pausing briefly at the front desk. Then he and Morgan went to the latter's car, and drove to St. Buryan and to....?

CHAPTER 55

▼

CONFLICTING EMOTIONS

Her cheeks reddened by the cold air, Janet Miller walked slowly and somberly back to the hotel. Two days had passed since her second puzzling disappointing visit to St. Buryan—two days spent in numbed confusion, and with a rising sense of both annoyance and loss.

"Perhaps Sgt. Bailey is right," she began to think, as she sat at her table, and toyed with her meal. She had no real interest in eating, these past two days. In fact, she seemed interested in very little, just now—except, perhaps, coming to grips with an unpleasant reality.

"It's all over, I suppose," she finally told herself. "It would be useless to continue brooding over it, or to deny it."

She shrugged her shoulders, and leisurely stirred her stew.

"Our friendship is dead—I may as well admit it," she told herself. "There's nothing left to do but bury it."

A trace of a sob escaped her lips. With it, she would begin her effort to let her memories of Gwen, and of their friendship, fade from her conscious mind.

She awoke next morning with conflicting feelings—she felt a certain emptiness caused by the loss of a once-treasured friendship, yet at the same time felt that a great weight had lifted from her.

She had just finished breakfast when she heard a woman's voice call her name. It was a voice that she had not expected to hear again.

She turned.

"Gwen? What are you doing here?" she asked, her voice trembling ever so slightly. She needed a minute to overcome this strange surprise—Gwen was the last person she thought would be visiting her.

"It's one of life's ironies, I suppose," Gwen replied. "Perhaps I felt that I owe you a clearer explanation for my recent decision—for my change of heart regarding our friendship. Perhaps I wanted to see you, and speak with you once more before you leave."

"Very well, Gwen," Janet replied, still defensive and aloof.

This visit caught her off-guard—how should she react to it?

She gestured towards an empty chair. "Would you care to join me?"

"No—no, thanks. I was hoping that we might talk in more private surroundings. Do you feel up to a drive to Maidenwell? It's a short drive. My car is outside—it would be no bother at all."

Conflicting emotions raced through Janet's mind. She felt wary, and confused. What did Gwen want?

"If that's what you want," Janet finally agreed. "Let me get my things. I shan't be long." So saying, she went to her room for her coat, scarf, gloves, and handbag.

Gwen Woodson smiled as they walked to her car, and got in.

They covered the first two miles in awkward silence. "It's a pity you won't get to see much of Cornwall—the real Cornwall," Gwen finally said.

"A pity? Why? What is the 'real' Cornwall?"

A look of almost mystical pride came to Gwen's face. "Psychically, this is the oldest, richest part of Britain," she began. "In fact, it's one of the foremost astral locales in the world. Great forces link our shrines with other sensitive points around the globe—the Great Pyramid, and Easter Island, for example."

Janet frowned. Gwen's speech disturbed her. Before she could comment, they pulled into the drive of the Woodsons' home in Maidenwell.

The two women got out of the car. As they approached the cottage, the front door opened. Jim Woodson stepped out.

"Back safely, are you?" he asked, as he gave his wife a passionless kiss on the cheek.

"Yes. How are the children?" she asked, as she returned the kiss.

"No problem," he replied, as they entered the house. Their puzzled guest followed at a slow, wary pace.

"Can I get you something?" Gwen offered.

"Yes, I think so," was the reply, with a trace of nervousness. "I'd like some answers, if you don't mind—to some puzzling questions."

Gwen lit a cigarette, as her husband poured drinks. She invited Janet to a place on the sofa. The same strange look that she had worn earlier now returned.

"Ours is a very old, very revered culture," she began. "The path we tread reaches far back into Britain's primordial beginnings—a pristine, sylvan age. It was a time of great psychic sensitivity. Our ancestors were in total astral accord with the cosmos, and with the great, vibrant power that flows through our land."

"In that most blessed age, our people were guided by the Druidh," her husband added.

Janet looked at him. He seemed less antagonistic than before. Why?

"Assisted by the filidh, and by a class of priests known as the Barddh, the Druidh were the conservators of a rich tradition," he continued. They were our seers, teachers, priests—the repositories of wisdom, and masters of the mysteries of the universe."

Poor Janet stared at them in mute, wide-eyed wonder. Why were they telling her this peculiar tale? How could it be of any concern to her?

Her questions, and her confusion, were clearly written on her face. "Why tell me about it?"

"Because Jim and I, and our friends, have been reborn into this timeless tradition," Gwen replied, in a tone of awe and reverence. "We've joined a sacred circle, and have been initiated into the way of the ancient mysteries."

"In three days, we will gather at one of the monuments built by the first Druids," the man added, solemnly and eagerly. "I'd like you to come with us, as we mark the end of the sacred cycle to see for yourself something of the way we've chosen. Then, you may understand why Gwen chose to end her friendship with you," he said, in an unusually pleasant manner.

"They're daft," Janet thought to herself, as her eyes shifted from one to the other. "Pristine mysteries? Psychic sensitivity? They are daft."

This strange revelation, and equally odd invitation, left her even more perplexed than before. And yet, that very strangeness piqued her healthy curiosity—that same quality that leads many into areas that are best left alone.

CHAPTER 56

▼

THROWING DOWN THE GAUNTLET

Eliezer Jordan felt a faint sense of foreboding as he followed Malcolm Morgan over the threshold of the latter's home. Once inside, he halted. His nose twitched nervously as he looked around and tried to get a feel for his new surroundings. Several minutes passed before he saw fit to lower his guard slightly.

His host took their coats, and put them away. "Care for a drink?" he asked.

Jordan shook his head.

Just then, Alice Morgan entered the room. She paused for a minute, and studied the newcomer. His presence raised a silent question in her mind.

"Is he the hailstone I saw?" she wondered. "If so, we're playing a dangerous game."

"Ah—Alice," Morgan greeted his wife. "Won't you join us?

This is Mr. Jordan, the man Ellen and Andrew told us about." Jordan and the woman exchanged nods.

"And now, Mr. Jordan, how can we help you," Morgan asked him, as they sat around a low, handcrafted table. "What would you like to know?"

Jordan waited before answering. He was busy studying the room's decor.

"All the furniture hand-made?" he asked.

"Yes. I made much of it myself, with some help here and there from some friends," Morgan replied, with some pride.

"And that?" asked Jordan, pointing to something on another table. "It looks like some sort of board game."

"It is. In fact, it's one of several I created."

Morgan walked over to a cabinet, and returned with several samples of his handiwork. "Each is based on a theme from Celtic folklore and mythology," he explained. "The one you're looking at is the 'Battle of Mag Tured.' One side are the Tuata de Dana—'The People of the Goddess Dana.' On the other are the Fomor, led by Balor of the Baleful Eye."

Jordan nodded noncommittally, as his host opened another box.

"This one comes from another famous tale—'Bran the Blessed.'"

Jordan studied the board, and the pieces. "Hmm. Yes—very curious," his hosts heard him mutter.

"What is it? Has something caught your interest?" asked Alice, speaking for the first time.

"Yes," Jordan replied, displaying a mild enthusiasm. "There is something—and it seems to be related to one of my questions."

"Really? What is it?"

Jordan pointed to something on the board. "These seven men here— what are they carrying? It looks like a head on a platter," he noted.

"Indeed it is," Morgan readily told him. "It's part of a most interesting tale. Would you care to hear it?"

Jordan nodded. For the next few minutes, he listened as his host told him the story of Bran.

Morgan brought the tale to an end by saying, "Bran's loyal followers decapitated him after his death, and carried his head with them for eighty-seven years before burying it on the site now known as Ludgate Hill, in London."

Jordan rubbed his chin. "For what purpose, I wonder? Was there a purpose?"

"Yes, there was," Alice felt the urge to tell him. "Bran was a mighty warrior," she said, with some pride. "A great chieftain and fighter. His deeds and prowess were esteemed and praised by our hard-fighting ancestors. As he lay dying on the field of battle, he instructed his faithful followers to sever his head, and bury it on Ludgate Hill, facing south. There it was to stay, to guard the land and its people from invasion and conquest."

There was something strange in her demeanor as she spoke. One would think that she had known the old boy personally, and had shared his exploits with him.

"Now, sir," Morgan suggested. "You've heard the tale of one of our most renowned heroes. Would you mind telling us what brought you to St. Buryan?"

The two men studied each other solemnly. The moment of truth was here. They knew it. And Alice knew it—just as she now knew that this was the man she had seen in her vision.

"I'm doing some research on any 'mystery cults' from the ancient Near East that might have reached Britain," Jordan calmly replied. "In the course of my reading, I came across a passing reference to the Cult of the Severed Head. I was curious to learn something about it.

He paused briefly, then went on. "A set of circumstances led me to Mr. Barrett's doorstep. Neither he nor the woman with him could tell me anything about it. But you can, can't you, Mr. Morgan?"

"I? Why do you say that?"

"Don't play games with me, Mr. Morgan. Why did you come to Penzance, looking for me? Or tell me that Barrett had gone to see you, to tell you of my visit? Why did you insist that I return here with you? Or tell me that Barrett thought you could answer my questions?"

Morgan poured drinks, then lit a cigarette.

"I've no doubt that you can tell me something," Jordan added. "The question is—if, and what."

"The Cult of the Severed Head was a very revered part of the old religion," Alice finally volunteered. "It was practiced by our warriors, but was held in high regard by all our people."

"Our people were neither ghouls nor head-hunters," her husband added. "The victims were those who had been slain in combat—in inter-tribal battles, or against the Romans. The heads were taken from dead foes—never from the living."

"It was a sign of respect towards one's fallen foes," Alice told him. "The heads of slain enemies were prized and sacred trophies—not merely signs of one's prowess, but moreso a hallowed talisman, guarding the home against evil."

Jordan kept his feelings to himself. "What about today?" he asked. "Are there any signs of its reappearance?"

The Morgans looked at him in genuine surprise. Alice fidgeted a bit. Malcolm chuckled.

"Of the Cult?" said he. "I hardly think so. But the old religion—the way of the Druid—is still very much alive. There are several thousands of us—here in Britain, and in parts of Ireland and Brittany—who still study its great mysteries, preserve the ancient language, and keep alive the lore and truths of a bygone, innocent age."

Jordan said nothing, but the expression on his face clearly reflected the skepticism that he felt.

"It's obvious that you doubt," said Morgan, when he saw that look. "Doubt that there are great mysteries—that our wise ones probed and mastered them, and passed them on to us."

"Oh, there are many mysteries—you can be sure of that," Jordan readily replied. "Far more than can be imagined by some overgrown children prancing in bedsheets around Stonehenge."

"Really, now? Would you care—would you dare—to throw down the gauntlet?" Morgan asked, eagerly. "If so, there are many of us—myself included—who would gladly accept the challenge."

Morgan's words and tone had an irresistible appeal to Jordan. He smiled confidently. "In that case, consider it thrown."

CHAPTER 57

▼

REDUCING THE ODDS

Silent, tired, and moody, three men sat in a room of a Bodmin hotel. One of them sat with his eyes closed, and the tips of his fingers tapping gently together.

At last, John Kelly opened his eyes. Raising his eyebrows, he gazed at his two colleagues. "Well, gentlemen?" he asked, in a soft tone. "Has anyone any suggestions?"

"Suggestions? Slithering salamanders!" Clovis Hobbs impatiently exclaimed. "What can we suggest? Even if you're correct—that a murder will occur one night this week, and at some stone monument—how do we know where? Or when?"

"I must agree with you, Hobbs," said Ferguson. "After all, we have at least seven nights, and quite a few sites, to choose from. I daresay that the odds are very heavily against us."

"There are at least twenty thousand such sites," Kelly told him. "I learned as much last week, from Mr. Cardigan. So, if I'm correct, the odds are at least 140,000 to 1 against our picking the time and place of the next murder."

He rubbed his weary face thoughtfully. "Those odds are too heavy to suit me," he said. "What do you say to whittling them down a bit—making them a bit less awesome, and more manageable?"

"How?" asked Hobbs.

"You once wanted to be an antiquarian, Hobbs," Kelly replied. "Would you care to nominate a likely site?"

The challenge surprised him. "I can suggest three, now that you ask," he replied. "Trethevy Quoit, and the 'Hurlers' stone circle, both not far from here. And a site in Brittany known as Carnac."

It was now Kelly's turn to be surprised. He hadn't expected so precise an answer—and so quickly.

"Why?" he asked. "Any special reasons?"

"Yes. If I'm not mistaken, this case began with a killing here in Bodmin. The latest one, also, occurred here. Trehevy

Quoit and the 'Hurlers' are two great circles near Bodmin—on the southern fringes of Bodmin Moor."

"And the one in Brittany?" asked Ferguson, as he toyed with his pipe.

"An educated guess. I'm going on a vague similarity between the place-name and the name of Cernunnos. Do you recall those pictures that were sent to the Rev. Thomson?"

When Ferguson and Kelly continued to stare, Hobbs scowled peevishly. "It is only a guess, you understand—not an infallible prediction," he emphasized.

"Of course, Hobbs. We realize that," the Scot assured him. "And for all we know, you might be correct. The next few days should tell, one way or another."

He sighed, then filled and lit his pipe. "Now, which day—or night—will it be? Any ideas, Kelly?"

Kelly stood up and began to pace the room slowly. When he same to a halt, he looked at his friends.

"All things considered, I would say Wednesday or Thursday. Yes—I'm sure that it will be one of those two nights," he said, as he flexed his fingers anxiously.

"What makes you say that?" asked Ferguson.

"Last Sunday was the winter solstice. I was once told that it may have inspired the fearful Walpergisnacht—the night when, quite literally, all hell was believed to break loose."

"In that case, there should have been another death last Sunday," said Hobbs. "But there wasn't. Why do you think that one may occur on one of the nights you named?"

"You're right, Hobbs. But we don't know if nothing happened. Remember that some of the bodies weren't found immediately after the murders. Now, Wednesday night is New Year's eve, and one of the last days of the year with the most hours of darkness. If it is chosen, it could be for either or both of these reasons," Kelly explained.

Ferguson smiled wanly. "Perhaps. Either way, we ought to ring Bailey to share our thoughts with him, and suggest appropriate action."

He picked up the phone, and began to dial. Then, a sharp knock on the door brought his hand to a halt. "Who is it?" he asked.

"Bailey," replied a rich baritone voice.

As the Scot put down the phone, Hobbs got up to let their caller in. "Your arrival is most timely," he said. "We were just about to ring you."

"Oh? Why?" asked Bailey, as he helped himself to a cup of tea.

Kelly gave him a concise summary of their discussion.

"You're right, Inspector," said Bailey. "The odds are staggering."

"Now, what brings you here?" Kelly naturally wondered.

"I'm off to Maidenwell again," Bailey the reply, with a grimace of annoyance.

"Maidenwell? Why?" asked Ferguson. "We've already been there."

Three pairs of eyes stared anxiously at the Cornishman.

Bailey drew a deep breath, and let it out slowly. "No, there hasn't been another one," he said, correctly reading their expressions. "Not yet, at least. And I want to keep it that way."

"Well?! What is it?" Kelly insisted.

"It seems that Miss Janet Miller is missing—and has been, for two days."

The three men looked at him in disbelief. "Janet Miller?! Disappeared? Are you sure?" they insisted.

"The proprietor of a local guest-house just rang us," Bailey told them. "One of his guests checked in early Wednesday afternoon. Thursday morning, a woman came to see her. The two of them sat and chatted for a few minutes, then got up and left. She didn't say where she was going. She hasn't been seen or heard from, since."

An angry Kelly slapped his thigh. "Damn dear Mother Mac-Farland!" he snapped.

"Let me come with you, Sergeant," Hobbs insisted. "I can't help feeling that she is my responsibility."

"Very well, Inspector," said Bailey. "Do you mind, gentlemen?" he asked Ferguson and Kelly.

Kelly scowled, and cursed under his breath.

"Mind?! Of course I mind! As if our problem weren't serious enough!"

"I suppose we do mind," replied Ferguson, a bit calmer than Kelly. "But it can't be helped, I imagine. We'll wait here until you return, or until you call us for help," he added, with a weak smile.

CHAPTER 58

▼

THE DUEL BEGINS

"You brought him home?! And you're going to bring him to the gathering?! Malcolm, I can't believe it. Are you daft?!"

Andrew Barrett was beside himself with anger and amazement.

"Why?" he asked, after pouring drinks for the two of them. "What's to be gained or proven by it?"

"Gained?" Morgan repeated, in a sinister calm. "Why—the elimination of a dangerous nuisance. That should be sufficient, shouldn't it?" he asked.

Barrett's face wore an expression that blended fear, mistrust, hatred, and confusion, in more or less equal amounts.

"I think you're making a mistake, Malcolm," he said. "It's an unnecessary risk—perhaps even a foolish one. Why? Has our luck been too good for you?"

"Why? Because he's there," Morgan forcefully replied; he was obviously annoyed that such a question had been asked, and that the normally self-assured Barrett should now have become so nervous, almost downright fearful.

"You've always been cautious, Andrew, but this anxiety is quite unlike you," Morgan observed, with a disapproving frown. "It seems uncalled-for, all things considered."

"What of your foolhardiness?" Barrett sternly replied. "Is that called for? If this man is on to us—if he is who and what you think—you may have bitten off far more than any of us can chew. We may well choke on this mouthful."

Clearly tense, Barrett lit a cigarette, and smoked part of it with a notice-able vehemence. "I hope you know what you're doing, Malcolm. We've been exceptionally lucky thus far. Let's not press that luck," Barrett advised him.

The druid wore an eager expression on his stern face. "Don't worry," he said, confidently. "In two days, the cycle will end. Then, next week at this time, we can proceed with our other plans. And the police will be none the wiser."

With this certainty, Morgan left and walked the short distance home through the brisk air. He arrived to find his guest rummaging through some books with an aloof curiosity.

"Pardon the absence. I had some business which couldn't wait," said Morgan. Jordan looked up from the book in his hand, and nodded in silent understanding.

"What do you find so interesting?" Morgan asked. His demeanor was now far more relaxed and friendly than it had been, just a short while earlier.

"This guide to the monoliths of Europe," Jordan replied.

"You seem fascinated by the material," Morgan rather vainly commented.

"Fascinated? No, not really," was the simple, matter-of-fact reply. "British folklore and archaeology aren't among my interests. But I **am** curious to know who built them—and how, and why. That is, if anybody really knows."

Morgan's eyes lit up. Almost instinctively, he sensed an opportunity to pick up the gauntlet that Jordan had thrown down a short while earlier.

"The answers to your questions exist—I can guarantee that," Morgan readily assured him.

"There may be 'answers,' Mr. Morgan," Jordan politely noted. "But what are they? And where, how, and by whom are they to be found?"

"I'm quite ready to show you the answers," Morgan confidently told him. "After all, I accepted your challenge. Are you willing to see and accept our great truths for yourself?"

Jordan could not help but smile. "Of course I'd like to see them," he replied, with a nod. "That is, if they exist. Lead on, MacDuff."

With a firm, eager step, he retrieved his coat, and put it on. Very keenly, and with a healthy skepticism, he followed his host, and embarked on the next phase of his strange adventure.

CHAPTER 59

▼

THE ANCIENT SIGNPOSTS

Morgan and the American had not gone very far when Morgan guided the car to the side of the road. Without a word, the to men got out, and gazed at the rolling, windswept countryside.

"There's no place like it in all England," Morgan observed, with pride. "I'd venture to say that it has no equal in all the world," he said, with a smile of satisfaction on his strong features.

Eliezer Jordan, who had seen many lands, said nothing. He simply studied his surroundings, and listened to the Cornishman.

"We're proud that Cornwall has always been last in many things," Morgan continued. "It was the last part of Britain to be Romanised, Anglicised, Chritianised, and industrialised. The ways of our noble ancestors have survived here with a great tenacity. The language, religion, poetry—all found a haven here, as successive invaders tried to eliminate us throughout the rest of the land."

Now, he led the way, as they walked a short distance along the road. They went through an opening of a fence, and halted at the edge of a pasture.

"This is one of the smaller stone circles of Cornwall," he explained. "It's called the 'Merry Maidens.' And over that low hill are two stones known as the 'Pipers'."

This was Jordan's first visit to any of Britain's stone circles. Ever curious, he walked around the ancient structure.

"Is the answer here?" he asked Morgan. "Or elsewhere?"

"It's here—and at a thousand other sacred sites," Morgan assured him. "A great cosmic force flows beneath our primeval soil. Its existence, and its nature, were discovered by the

Druids, the ancient teachers, priests, and seers of our race. They found that this wondrous power flows through a network of channels, known as ley lines. They oversaw the erection of monoliths at special points along those lines—points at which they could tap into that power, and utilize it."

"Are there other such places in Cornwall?" Jordan asked. "Any groups devoted to this culture? To the old religion?"

"There are several still-sacred, still-used sites throughout the shire," Morgan told him, as they returned to the car, and drove on. "We're now going to Cairn Euny, just north of St. Buryan. The circles of Lanyon Quoit and Chysauster are near Penzance. And Trethevy Quoit and the 'Hurlers' are near Bodmin moor."

Once again, he stopped the car, not far from another mute relic of a distant, unknown past.

"Here in Britain, and across the Channel in Brittany, many have preserved the ways of our ancestors. Our druidic circles have rescued our heritage from oblivion. We safeguard it, and are sustained and enriched by it," Morgan explained.

"Hmm. I see. Do you meet at sites like this one?" asked Jordan, as he viewed the small ring of stones known as the '

'Merry Maidens.'

"Yes. We meet four times each year, to mark the four major points of the Celtic calendar. There are also several lesser gatherings throughout the year."

"I might almost be interested in seeing one," Jordan mused.

"That can easily be arranged," Morgan replied, with a some enthusiasm. "Tuesday evening, the druidic circles will gather at several such sites—as part of the rites of the winter solstice, to insure the sun's rebirth."

"Indeed?" asked Jordan, with some keenness. "I'd like to see it—unless, of course, outsiders aren't permitted."

"As a rule, they aren't. All too often, they view us as oddities. But we'd be most happy to welcome you. I can promise you an honoured place, when we mark the sun's renewal," said Morgan.

CHAPTER 60

▼

"LET'S GET ON WITH IT"

Shortly after sunrise, John Kelly got out of bed. When his two colleagues awoke, they saw him going through a series of odd motions.

"What ever are you doing?" asked Mr. Hobbs, at the end of that strange ritual.

"Sharpening my wits—loosening my joints and limbs—keeping my mind and body supple," was the reply, in a pleasant, regal tone.

"How?"

"By a mixture of yoga, t'ai chi, and isometrics. You really should try it—it works wonders for me."

"We could use a wonder or two, just now," Ferguson quietly noted. "We've a new day ahead. Let's use it wisely."

After a simple breakfast, the men from Scotland Yard returned to police headquarters. They had just begun to plan a strategy when Sgt. Bailey joined them.

"Well? Did you find her?" asked John Kelly, after Bailey removed his coat and sat down.

"Perhaps," Bailey replied, as Ferguson handed him a mug of warm cocoa. He held the cup between his hands, and gazed at it intently. But his thoughts were obviously elsewhere. After a brief, pensive silence, he spoke again.

"Apparently, Miss Miller returned to Bodmin on Wednesday, and paid another call on her one-time friend," he began. He paused, and drank some cocoa.

"Thursday morning, Mrs. Woodson drove to Bodmin, and called on her. They sat and talked for a few minutes, then got up and left together— back to Maidenwell, I assume."

He ran his strong fingers through his bushy hair.

"Miss Miller didn't take her suitcase with her, nor did she check out of the quest-house. And she hasn't been back from Maidenwell since Thursday," he told them.

"Did you learn anything?" Kelly asked. "Notice anything out of the ordinary?"

"Yes. I noticed several peculiar things," said Bailey, as he leaned forward and rested his forearms on his desk.

"Hobbs has already noted one—why did Miss Miller return to Bodmin? She knew that you were coming here—why work at cross-purposes? Or risk getting in our way? Why return, after Mrs. Woodson had clearly ended their friendship? And why, having ended it, did Mrs. Woodson decide to call on here, three days ago?"

"And invite her to stay with her, as her house-guest?" asked Ferguson, picking up his train of thought.

"Why were the Woodson's far less defensive and tight-lipped than on my two previous visits?" Bailey added. "I'll wager that they know a great deal. They may be concealing something, or shielding someone, for all we know."

The others understood his suspicion. But they had no tangible evidence with which to tie the Woodsons—or anyone else, for that matter— to any wrongdoing.

"What do we do, now?" Bailey wondered.

"Two of us should visit Rev. Thomson," Kelly suggested. "And two go to the home of the man who was killed last Saturday—learn as much as we can, from those who knew him."

His friends nodded in ready agreement.

"We must also find the driver who tried to kill the vicar," he added. "He could be a source of valuable information."

Bailey needed no urging on that score. In fact, he had begun the search shortly after the accident.

"And I would suggest a discrete surveillance of the Woodson home," said Ferguson. "It might prove rewarding."

"Very well," said Bailey, "let's get on with it. Who'll go with me to Helland?"

CHAPTER 61

▼

A NIGHT TO REMEMBER

Tuesday afternoon waxed and waned, but its ebbing did not go unnoticed. Indeed, its passing had been eagerly anticipated, and ardently awaited.

In various parts of Britain, and on the Continent, thousands of people were gathering many sacred ritual objects together. They would meet on this cold winter's night, at hundreds of ancient sites—at monoliths, circles, henges, and cairns. All were followers of pre-Christian paganism, and were meeting at these hallowed sites to perform a task of sadness and joy, of despair and hope.

One week ago, on the night of the winter solstice, the sun had died. It had to be renewed, lest all life perish from the face of the earth.

The winter solstice. A time viewed with awe and dread since the dawn of human consciousness.

At Stonehenge and Avebury, at Newgrange and Chysauster, at Carnac and La Tene, and at hundreds of equally ancient monuments, they now came together, in a most solemn, sober, and reverent manner.

In Cornwall, as elsewhere, loyal adherents of the old ways were piously converging around several ancient locations. With their ritual garb—long, flowing robes; sphinx-like coverings over their heads and shoulders; pendants etched with pentacles and other magical symbols—they approached the sacred sites.

From St. Buryan and St. Ives they were coming—from Penzance, Bodmin, and other communities. And the 'Keepers of the Ley Lines' were preparing to mark this great and awesome event with the blood of a human sacrifice.

In a cottage in St. Buryan, Eliezer Jordan had been looking forward to this evening with considerable interest and enthusiasm. This was what he had been waiting for—working and hoping for—these past twelve days.

"Too bad Ferguson and Kelly aren't here to enjoy the fun," he thought to himself, with a wry smile. "Well, I'll have to save some of the cake for them," he promised himself, as he went with the Morgans for the short ride to the cairn.

The night was still quite young when the last of nearly one hundred people arrived. Eliezer Jordan, ever an alert observer, took careful note of everything around him.

What was he to make of this most peculiar assemblage? Of the mystifying ritual that he was being allowed to witness?

Why was Malcolm Morgan so anxious to have him here this particular evening? Why had he promised a warm welcome at this pagan rite for one who had openly doubted the validity of the Cornishman's cherished beliefs?

Why had Morgan shared so freely of his knowledge with him?

And insisted on having Jordan as his houseguest?

Why had Alice Morgan become open and friendly this afternoon, after having been so cold and cross since his arrival?

An eerie silence now hung over the cairn, and over the grim and solemn assembly. Four of the celebrants took out small musical instruments—a pair of cymbals, a lyre, a cornet, and two small drums.

The musicians placed themselves at regular intervals around the cairn. Four others now stepped forward, each carrying a sizeable wicker basket. From his vantagepoint, Jordan saw that they were duplicates of the one he had seen in his dream, and the one that had been left in the church in Bodmin, a week ago.

The outsider scowled, and looked intently around him. His eyes came to a halt when they saw one young woman. Something about her caught his attention as he sensed that she, like himself, didn't belong there.

Despite the chill in the air, he removed his coat. He reached into the tote bag that he always carried with him.

None paid any attention to him as he removed three objects—a woolen skullcap, a prayer shawl, and a pendant. His wife and eldest daughter had knitted the prayer shawl and skullcap for his last birthday; the teacher who had guided him in his initial study of the Kabbalah had given the pendant to him.

For an instant, he looked at the pendant—a finely polished slice of stone the size of his palm. On its face an ancient symbol—the Kabbalistic Tree of Life—had been etched. As he looked at it, he reflected for a moment.

He put the skullcap on. Then, saying the appropriate prayers, he put on the prayer shawl and pendant.

Scarce had done so when two of the celebrants approached him, and two others walked up to the frightened young woman. Guided by some strange sense of cosmic duty, they led their reluctant guests to the center of the circular area.

Fear and apprehension now overcame the woman. The faint memory of something that Kelly had told her, so long ago and far away, began to sound very faintly in the back of her mind, and added to her anxiety. The sight of three people—her former friend among them—holding sacrificial knives did nothing to soothe her taut nerves.

Their guards bound the wrists of Jordan and the girl with lengths of silver cord. Miss Miller was sobbing uncontrollably as she and her companion in horror became the focal points of this bizarre ritual.

As those around them chanted their incantations, two men and women stepped forward; they led Jordan and the girl forward, offering strange libations to strange, dark forces, as they walked.

Eliezer Jordan said and did nothing. Effortlessly, he withdrew into himself. His heartbeat and breathing were slowing down. By the time the four marchers had come to a halt, and the assembly had ceased its obscene chanting, he seemed already dead.

A woman with a sacrificial knife approached the victims. It was Gwen Woodson. This was the moment that she had long been waiting for—with this sacrifice, she would cross the line from postulant to priestess.

Her whole being pulsated with a fervent joy. What did it matter that her former friend and this inquisitive stranger had to die, for her to gain this honor? Who were they to her? Of what consequence their puny lives compared to the goal to be attained? To their duty of resurrecting the great solar orb?

With a great solemn joy, and a festive sense of awe and duty, she neared the two chosen offerings from one side. Equally solemn, Alice Morgan approached from the other. In her hands, she held a large wicker basket, in which a wreath of mistletoe rested.

Regally garbed in their priestly raiment, three men approached—Malcolm Morgan, followed by James Woodson and Andrew Barrett. The former raised his staff of office, and addressed the intended victims.

"Imbue the soil of Albion with your ebbing lives. Become one with its wondrous forces—flow through the life-giving ley lines, and feed its mystic currents. Those who inquired where they did not belong shall remain here forever. He who mocked the revered secrets will now witness them, and become their servant."

Triumphantly—contemptuously—Morgan looked at the two who were about to die. He breathed deeply, and savored his moment of triumph.

Then, the transformation took place.

As a hundred incredulous onlookers watched, an unkown force began to emanate from he who had been Eliezer Jordan. Those around him were struck dumb with fear and astonishment. They tried to turn and flee, but could not move.

The source of this power now opened his eyes. No longer was he Eliezer Jordan, teacher and scholar. He was now Barad—the mysterious—the inscrutable.

Silently, he looked around him. An enigmatic smile came to his face as he broke the bonds on his wrists. He placed a hand on his pendant. Drawing a few long, deep breaths, he began to pray.

The once-clear skies became overcast, as the area around Cairn Euny was hit by a most unexpected hailstorm.

A great consternation spread quickly through the assembly, like fire through dry brush. Overcoming their initial paralysis, they dropped their sacral objects, and turned to flee in a hundred different directions.

It was then that the cry of "Everybody halt! We're the police!" echoed across the ageless ground.

The echoed had hardly faded when even Barad himself was surprised. Quietly, he smiled. Then, he held out an arm to support the woman, who fainted from shock. Gently, he lowered her to the ground, and placed a fatherly hand on her lifeless face.

"Good—she'll live," he finally assured himself. Then, he sat down next to her, and closed his eyes. His head dropped slowly forward, and he fell into a deep, refreshing sleep.

CHAPTER 62

▼

THE PUZZLE EXPLAINED

The sun was already up when Eliezer Jordan awoke on Wed-nesday morning. Consciousness seemed to come to him with some reluctance, that day. Slowly, a pair of strong hands reached up, and rubbed his tired face. Like a mangy lion, he shook his head, sat up, and opened his eyes.

His alert, pale blue eyes studied the hotel room, as he knitted his brow in mild bewilderment. Then, he stood up, and washed and dressed. As he prepared to go downstairs, he found a noted taped to the telephone.

"Welcome to Penzance," it began. "Thanks for leading us on a merry chase. Hope you've had a pleasant nap. Meet us at police station."

It was signed by John Kelly.

Jordan smiled a warm smile as he put the note in his pocket and went off to meet his two friends. Greetings were warm and sincere when he entered the Penzance police station and stood with them once more.

"Well, gentlemen," he asked, as their feelings of excite-met and relief subsided somewhat. "What took you so long? Where have you fellows been, these past few days?"

He shook his head in mock dismay.

"I'm glad you bothered to show up when you did—I was afraid you'd miss all the fun," he added, as they all enjoyed a hearty laugh.

A very perplexed local chief constable looked on, not knowing what to make of all this—of Bailey's cryptic phone-calls; of the urgent visit by Bailey and the three men from the Yard; and, most of all—that late-night trip to Cairn Euny, and its most unusual results.

"Listen here, Sergeant," he finally said. "I think that an explanation is in order. What was that all about? What does this Yank have to do with it? And what was that freak hail-storm?"

Jordan exchanged glances with Ferguson and Kelly, then looked understandingly at Constable Porter. "I appreciate your confusion, Constable," he assured the man. "I think that each of us can explain a different part of a strange and deadly puzzle—a deadly game that began with a murder in Bodmin, and ended last night."

"Very well, Professor," Kelly invited him. "Would you care to begin? How did you identify this 'cult of the severed head' as the culprit? How did you know that an attempt was made to kill Rev. Thomson?"

"Hmm. Let me see. Well, in retrospect, it all seems quite simple," Jordan began. "Though at the time, it was most perplexing. First—there was a series of dreams that I had. Two were of a stone pillar with a human head carved on it, and blood oozing from it.

"Second was of Jonah being swallowed by a large fish. The third was from an ancient Egyptian creation-myth. And the fourth was of a wicker basket containing a wreath of mistletoes, and a pair of hands and feet— just what you found in Rev. Thompson's study, Sgt. Bailey."

The policemen listened in mute disbelief.

"Initially, I could make no sense at all of any of it. The meaning finally came to me this past week-end, when I went to see the Cardigans," he continued. "First, I had a dream in which I saw two Hebrew letters whose numerical value is ninety-five. Then, I heard the first two words of the 95th Psalm. That's what pointed me towards the solution."

"Psalms? Jonah? Egyptian myths? You make it sound even more con-fusing," Porter commented.

"I'm sorry. Well—when Jonah was thrown overboard, he was on his way to Nineveh. 'Nineveh' begins with the Hebrew letter NUN meaning 'fish'—and Jonah was swallowed by a 'great fish.' And NUN, in the mythology of ancient Egypt, represented the primordial waters of cre-ation," he explained.

"What of the 95th Psalm?" asked Hobbs.

"The Psalm? Well, that's easy to explain—now. The opening words, in Hebrew, are 'L'choo n'ran'nah le'Shem.' The English translation means, more or less, 'Come, let us sing unto the Lord; let us make a joyful noise to the Rock of our salvation.'

"The Hebrew word 'n'ran'nah' means 'let us sing.' In the Kabbalah, the letters nun-resh-nun form an acronym. They're the initial letters of the Hebrew words nefesh, ruach, neshamah—the three levels of the soul, which dwells in the head. That, together with my dreams—and the fact that three victims had been decapitated—led me to ask Mr. Cardigan about the importance of the head among the ancient Celts."

He paused, and drew a deep breath. "Anything else?"

"How did you know about Rev. Thomson's accident?" asked Ferguson.

"I didn't. But from what I had heard—especially after I spoke with the Cardigans—I suspected that those sketches, and the mutilated corpse, were meant as a warning. I called to advise caution, not to make a prediction."

He stood up, stretched his limbs, then asked, "How did you know where I was? And that I might be in trouble? Or when and where to come to help me?"

"A lot of work, and a little bit of luck," said Bailey. "First, we found the man who tried to kill the vicar. He wasn't too talkative, but he said enough. We arrested him on a charge of attempted murder."

"A visit to Helland revealed something about the man who had been killed on Saturday—the one whose body had been left in the church,"

Ferguson added. "He had been a member of the 'Keepers of the Ley Lines.' He apparently tried to leave them after the murders began."

"I see. But how did you manage to show up at the right place, and the right time?"

John Kelly answered that. "We can thank our friend Mr. Cardigan for that. He rang us early yesterday afternoon to tell us where you had gone, and why. He was quite worried—even wanted to come along and help."

"He told us that some druidic circles were holding some rites Tuesday evening," Bailey added. "His own would be at Tintagel. Since you had gone to St. Buryan, we naturally decided to look for you at the nearest pre-historic monument, which was Cairn Euny."

Tired and relieved, Jordan shook his head. "What about the girl?" he asked. "Where is she? How is she?"

"She's in the hospital," Constable Porter told him. "Suf-fering from shock and exhaustion. Doctors say that it will be a fortnight or so before she's back on her feet."

"Could I see her before I leave?" a concerned Jordan asked.

"I suppose so. Naturally, we'll have to check with the doctors, first."

Jordan nodded. Then, he looked at his two friends. "I guess that settles it," he said, with a sigh of relief. "I ought to go to St. Ives now—I want to return the Cardigans' car, and thank them for their help. I'll see you in London tomorrow. It's been nice meeting you," he assured Sgt. Bailey, as they exchanged a firm handshake. "Please give my best to the vicar. Constable Porter—thanks for your very timely help."

CHAPTER 63

▼

TIME FLIES

Early Sunday afternoon, three men and a woman emerged from a car at the Gatwick Airport car-park. They went to the departure area, and one of the men checked his bags.

"Good-bye, Mr. Kelly—we've run a good course together," he said, as he and his friend shook hands.

"Good enough, I should think," said the detective. "By the way, Professor, I have one more question, if you don't mind."

"Not at all. What is it?"

"Your first day here, when you went to the Museum with Mr. Cardigan, how were you able to communicate? After all, you don't speak the Celtic language. And he spoke no English until you went to that 'lecture.'"

"Oh—that," said Jordan, with a chuckle. "Do you remember your Sherlock Holmes?"

"A little. Why?"

"Watson often referred to Holmes's many monographs. One of them was 'The Chaldean Roots of the Ancient Cornish Language.' Conan

Doyle probably never knew how right he was. I don't speak Gaelic, but I do speak Akkadian. When Cardigan began to speak to me in his own language, I detected a marked similarity between it and Akkadian. The similarity was enough to allow us to communicate with very little diffi-culty."

"No! Really?!"

"Yes—really," was the reply, with a smile.

"Well, bless dear Mother MacFarland."

"Good-bye, Peggy," Jordan then said to the woman, as they exchanged warm smiles. "I'm sorry that my visit had to be under such grim circumstances. Perhaps some day soon, you'll come for a visit to my side of the ocean."

"I'd like that," she agreed. "And under friendlier conditions."

"Good-bye, Mr. Ferguson," he said, as he and the Scot shook hands. "I can't thank you enough for calling me. These past two weeks have been most interesting," he said, with a warm smile.

"Good-bye, Professor. You're the finest detective of us all." It was then that they heard the announcement for his flight.

The friends shared another quick, warm farewell; Jordan repeated his invitation, then turned and headed for his plane.

Seven hours later, his plane touched the tarmac at Newark Airport. Once through Customs, he hailed a cab, and was soon back at that familiar house in Madison. He fumbled for his keys, then let himself in.

"Who's there?" a woman called from upstairs. "Benjy? Dinah?"

"Nope. Just me," was his quiet reply, as he dropped his two small bags. A pair of feet tripped easily down the stairs.

"Oh dear—Luzzy!" Naomi Jordan gasped in genuine sur-prise. "Well!" she chided him, as she quickly regained her composure.

"It's been two weeks, Luzzy. Two weeks, and not even a postcard," she said, as her dark frown easily turned into a bright smile.

The tired man raised his eyebrows. "That long? How time flies, when you're having fun."

Then, he took her in his arms, and gave her a long loving kiss.

ABOUT THE AUTHOR

Bruce Salen is a send-generation Brooklynite and a fifth-generation New Yorker.

His interest in mystery fiction began at the age of 9, when he first started reading the HARDY BOY books.

His interest in ancient history and archaeology began when he was 11 or 12. This interest was kindled in part by a teacher, Dr. Joseph Kaster, who was an Egyptologist, and in part by four books that he had discovered at his local public library:-MOUNTAINS OF PHAROAH and LOST PHAROAHS, both by Leonard Cottrell; and GODS, GRAVES, AND SCHOLARS and SECRET OF THE HITTITES, both by C.W. Ceram.

This interest in the ancient Near East led him to do some graduate study at NYU in the area of Biblical literature; his interest in archaeology led him to work as a volunteer on two digs in Israel–Tel Dan, in 1976, and Ashekelon, in 1996.

His other interests include scuba-diving (he got his initial certification in the summer of 1993), and amateur radio (he got his Novice ticket in

December 1994, and is KB2SUR, and a member of the Kings County Radio Club).

The author lives in his native Brooklyn, and would like to acknowlege his parents and grandparents, for their constant patience and guidance on the road of life, and his agent, Jim Schiavone, for his patience, and for his confidence both in him and in his writing. Thanks, Jim.